REDEMPTION OF THE UNTAMED ITALIAN

CLARE CONNELLY

MILLS & BOON

First published in Great Britain 2020
by Mills & Boon, an imprint of HarperCollins*Publishers*
1 London Bridge Street, London, SE1 9GF

Large Print edition 2020

© 2020 Clare Connelly

ISBN: 978-0-263-08461-0

MIX
Paper from
responsible sources
FSC™ C007454

This book is produced from independently certified
FSC™ paper to ensure responsible forest management. For
more information visit www.harpercollins.co.uk/green.

Printed and bound in Great Britain
by CPI Group (UK) Ltd, Croydon, CR0 4YY

To you, a reader of romance,
a lover of love.
This book—and every book I write—
is because of you.

PROLOGUE

HE WASN'T SURE WHY, but Cesare paused outside the restaurant a moment, looking through the deep-glass windows at the elegant scene inside. The room was warmly lit, the crowd painfully fashionable.

He stood on the outside looking in and couldn't fail to appreciate the irony. As a child, he'd often been like this: standing outside rooms of wealth and privilege, kept physically distinct, separate from and unwanted by that world. Even as a teenager with a scholarship placement at the best school in England he'd felt outside the norm. He'd been different and everyone had known it. Unlike the sons of ancient, wealthy families who'd formed the student ranks, he'd been only the son of a poor single mother, a woman who'd served as a nanny to that kind of family.

Now, though, as he looked into the restaurant, he knew places like this existed for the likes of him. He would walk in and people would part as a wave, making way for him, admiring him, wanting his attention. He knew because it was what always happened these days.

He scanned the trendy 'it' spot until his eyes landed on his table. He recognised Laurence immediately, the man who was so desperate for Cesare to invest in his hedge fund he was practically at begging point. A dark smile tinted Cesare's lips. When he'd been a young boy thrown into the world of the British aristocracy, and seen as lesser than it in every way, he'd sworn he would make men of this ilk pay. He'd sworn he would be better, bigger, more successful always. He swore he would make his fortune and he swore he would make them pay.

His eyes slid unconsciously to Laurence's companion. Not his companion, his cousin, Cesare remembered, his smile turning mocking now. It was an obvious ploy to win Cesare's favour, or perhaps distract him from matters of business. His reputation as a womaniser was well-established and he was unapologetic for that. He liked women, different women and often. If Laurence thought having her at this dinner meeting would make an ounce of difference to Cesare's investment plans, he didn't understand the kind of fortitude and intention Cesare brought to his business life.

Jemima Woodcroft was every bit as beautiful in the flesh as all the billboards would have you believe, though. The supermodel leaned across to her cousin, speaking close to his ear, and Laurence nodded, laughing. She in turn smiled, and her eyes flashed with something that sparked a light of curiosity inside Cesare.

Something else, too. Desire.

She was just the kind of woman Cesare usually chose to take to bed: beautiful, sophisticated and, if the media reports were to be believed, as happy to employ a revolving door with her bed as he was with his. Her hand pulled her hair over one shoulder, and manicured fingers toyed with its length distractedly, so two vivid images leaped into his mind unbidden: her nails running down his body, pale fingers against tanned flesh and her hair forming a curtain around her face as she straddled him, looking down at him, her face tortured by passion.

Suddenly, the night was looking up.

He pushed into the restaurant with a sense

of anticipation. Like the steady beating of a drum, it filled his chest. The world was at Cesare's feet—he'd worked hard to make sure of that—and he doubted he'd ever grow tired of reaping the rewards.

CHAPTER ONE

'I STILL FIND it hard to see what's in it for me.'

Cesare Durante spoke with a voice that was naturally husky and deep, his accent ever so slightly Italian but also cultured and British. Jemima observed him from beneath shuttered lashes, wishing he hadn't so completely lived up to her expectations. Everything she'd read about the self-made billionaire had told her what he'd be like: intelligent but charming, with the kind of looks that would make almost anyone weak at the knees.

But there was an arrogance about him too, an arrogance that communicated itself with every curve of his lips, every flash of his sharp, perceptive eyes.

When he'd introduced himself even his name had dispelled any idea that there might be a lingering softness buried in his broadly muscled chest. 'Cesare,' he'd said, almost as a command, the pronunciation faithful to the Italian, so it sounded like 'Che-zar-eh'. From his lips it emerged as a rumble, a deep, rolling wave that crashed over Jemima and momentarily robbed her of breath.

'The fund's versatility is the main selling point,' Laurence interjected with a confidence she knew he didn't feel.

'If my investors find out I've tanked a third of the fund's value, I'm screwed, Jem. That's like a hundred million quid. I need to get Durante on side—it's the only way I can keep things afloat. Please help. Please.'

Even as a child she'd have done anything Laurence asked of her, but after her brother's death Laurence and Jemima had been bonded in that unique way grief conspired to bring about. Laurence was the only person who could understand the void in her life and, at the same time, he was the only person who could go halfway to filling it. They were family, they were friends, they were two souls who'd known intense loss and guilt, and she'd do anything he asked of her.

Just as he'd do anything for her. She knew that was why he'd made such irresponsible, reckless investments: to save Almer Hall. He knew the extent of debt her parents were in and that even her income wasn't equal to it. He was working himself into the ground, taking lavish risks, because he knew what the Hall meant to them and she loved him to bits for that.

'Most funds have a range of assets.' Cesare Durante's expression showed displeasure. 'I didn't fly in from Rome for a middling sales pitch. Tell me what else you've got.'

She felt Laurence's tension and her own stomach swirled. She hated seeing him like this, and she understood his anxiety. She knew what this meant to him. More importantly, she knew what would happen if Cesare Durante didn't invest in Laurence's hedge fund—financial ruin, certainly, and likely criminal charges for the reckless way he'd invested other people's money without advising them of his activities. He'd be ruined, absolutely, and by extension so would her parents, because Laurence would no longer be in a position to offer any financial help to them. They'd already lost so much and couldn't cope with another hurdle.

Reaching for her champagne, she held it just a few inches from her lips, her large green eyes regarding Cesare thoughtfully. Her eyes were one of Jemima's most recognisable features. The first international campaign she'd landed had been for a cosmetic giant and promoting mascara had launched her career globally. She trained the full force of those eyes on the Italian now, leaning forward slightly.

'Did you just fly in today?' She kept her tone light intentionally.

Laurence had been clear: *'With you there, it'll feel social. Fun. Keep the heat off me, distract him from how much cash I'm asking him to kick in.'*

Keeping the heat off with Cesare Durante at the table was apparently a physical impossibility. As he slowly turned to face her, her pulse kicked up a gear and her blood begin to boil in her veins. It took all her discipline to maintain a muted expression on her face.

'This evening.' His gaze shifted over her face in that same appraising way, as though he was studying her piece by piece.

It was impossible to be one of the world's most sought-after models without knowing yourself to be beautiful. Jemima accepted that there was something in the physical construction of her face and body that was widely regarded to be attractive, but she was very pragmatic about it. She knew that she couldn't take credit for any of these things—looks and beauty were almost entirely a question of chance, and as such the fact she was objectively beautiful gave her very little satisfaction. It was far easier to be proud of goals you worked hard to achieve rather than windfalls you were handed. She generally didn't think about her looks much at all, except in relation to her work, to trends she might need to emulate or embrace.

But as Cesare swept his thickly lashed eyes over her face and his wide lips—set in a perfectly square jaw—quirked a little, she felt an unwelcome rush of warmth and feminine satisfaction fill her chest. His gaze travelled to her lips, lingering there for so long they began to tingle, and a flash of something with which she had very little personal experience but still recognised burst through her—desire, unmistakable, overtook her body, warming her insides, making her breath burn in her lungs.

'And you?' He matched her body language, leaning forward a little so she was acutely conscious of his frame. There wasn't an ounce of spare flesh on him and yet somehow he seemed *huge*, as if he took up more than his allotment of physical space in the fashionable restaurant. He had to be six and a half feet, but it wasn't his size alone that was formidable. It was as though he'd been cast from stone, or sculpted from bronzed marble. His body was broad, his shoulders squared and strong, his waist slim where his shirt met the leather belt, his legs long and confident. He'd discarded his jacket some time after their main course plates had been cleared and the cotton shirt he wore underneath, though undoubtedly the very best quality, and likely hand-stitched specifically for his body, strained just a little at the tops of his arms, so she could see that his biceps were pronounced.

But it was his face that had fascinated her all evening. It too had the appearance of having been deliberately sculpted, but by a hand of exceptional talent. It was a symmetrical face, with an aquiline nose, a firm, chiselled jaw, thick dark lashes above intensely watchful eyes and lips that were wide and deliberate. And when he smiled—which he hadn't done much—two deep dimples scored his cheeks. His hair was thick and dark, cut close to his face, in contrast to a stubbled chin that she imagined would feel quite coarse beneath her fingertips.

Jemima was used to physical beauty. It didn't generally impress her. She spent much of her time surrounded by models and, if anything, she'd begun to crave interesting, unusual features: skin that was marked with lines or tattoos, faces that told stories and invited questions.

He was purely beautiful, and yet she was fascinated by him, intrigued by him. She sensed something within him that made her want to ask questions, that inflamed her curiosity.

'Jemima lives around the corner.' Laurence spoke for her at the same time he lifted a hand to call a waiter's attention. Neither Cesare nor Jemima looked away. It was as though they were the only people in the room.

'I have a flat,' she supplied after a beat.

One single brow lifted, changing his face altogether, so now she felt scepticism emanating from him. 'You grew up in London?'

'No.' She shook her head. 'My family has an estate outside of Yorkshire. Almer Hall.' She and Laurence shared a brief look at the mention of the family property that meant so much to them, the family property that would be lost if the hedge fund went down the drain.

Cynicism briefly converted to insolent mockery and then his expression was blank of anything except banal, idle curiosity.

'You're aristocracy.' It wasn't a question and yet she felt compelled to answer.

She lifted her shoulders. 'There's a title there somewhere. We don't use it.'

'Why not?'

'It feels a bit outdated.' She sipped her champagne now, relishing the popping of bubbles as they raced down her throat. His watchful gaze was warming her up, so she was glad for the cooling effect of the drink.

'Scotch, Cesare?' Laurence offered. Cesare finally took his attention from her and Jemima expelled all her breath in a long, quiet whoosh. She blinked, as though waking from a dream, and leaned back in her seat a little.

What would it be like to have those steel-grey eyes turned on her with the full force of his attention? No, she'd had his attention… With the full force of his desire? What would it be like to lean forward and brush her fingertips over his arm, to flirt with him a little, to smile and murmur an invitation in his ear?

Not for the first time, she felt the burden of her virginity with a burning sense of impatience. If she'd had some experience she'd be sorely tempted to act on those impulses. After all, the media had already hanged her for the crime of being a harlot—she might as well enjoy some of the spoils. Yes, if she'd had even a hint of experience she may well have acted on her impulse despite what that might mean for Laurence, despite the fact it could complicate matters for him.

Cesare's voice was deep as he said the name of a whisky she recognised only because it was one that a photographer friend favoured—it was outrageously overpriced. Laurence ordered the same but, before the waiter could be dispatched, Cesare turned back to Jemima; her pulse rushed.

'You are happy with your champagne?'

Her heart shifted in her chest. Despite all the reasons to maintain her distance, desire pushed her forward a little, just a fraction, as though her body was on autopilot, seeking his.

It was madness. As a teen model, she'd come

across more than her fair share of designers, photographers, magazine editors and public relations guys, all of whom had thought she'd do whatever it took to advance her career, so by her fifteenth birthday she'd become adept at saying no without causing offence. In fact, she was very good at saying no without even having people realise that she was rejecting them. Sex, drugs, alcohol, orgies. Jemima had a knack for turning people down and still having them think well of her.

But there was danger in Cesare—a darkness that called to her, that made her certain he could be her weakness, and in that moment she wished more than anything that she was the kind of woman the world thought her to be. She wished she was sophisticated and experienced and that she knew exactly what to say to get a man like Cesare to have sex with her.

The thought alone had her standing abruptly, scraping her chair back so both sets of eyes lifted to her.

'You okay?' Laurence queried.

'Perfectly fine.' She pasted a smile to her face as she became aware more people were looking in her direction. Cursing her recognisability, and the fact Laurence had chosen this celebrity hotspot in an attempt to impress his would-be investor, she nodded jerkily. 'I'll be right back.'

She forced herself to walk sedately towards the facilities. Once inside, she lingered with her back against the cold, marble wall and her eyes swept shut.

She'd likely never see Cesare Durante again after this night. She was there for one reason and one reason only: to help Laurence secure him as an investor.

She had to help her cousin—there was too much at stake to risk ruining the evening because she couldn't stop looking at Cesare and imagining what those broad, capable hands would feel like running over her body... Heat flushed her cheeks because she knew they'd feel good. Better than good. But that was beside the point—nothing was going to happen between them. She needed to get a grip.

Sucking in a deep breath, she quickly checked her appearance in the mirror, pausing just long enough to reapply her soft coral lipstick and finger-comb her generous, side-sweeping fringe so it artfully covered one eye. She sucked in a deep, fortifying breath and pulled the door inward, stepping into the wallpapered, dimly lit corridor that led to the amenities. At one end, there was a sideboard with a huge bunch of lilies sitting on top of it. A nostalgic smile briefly curved her lips.

As a child, Almer Hall had always had flowers. Huge arrangements, just like this, grand and fragrant. She paused in front of the vase, her fingertips lifting on autopilot to gently stroke the petals—like silk, dewy and tender. She inhaled the scent and swept her eyes shut, remembering the feeling of visiting her grandparents as a child, running down the marbled hallways. In summer, the fragrance had been almost overwhelming.

There were no flowers now. More than two-thirds of the house was shut down, doors closed, furniture—what remained of it—covered in sheets. The family quarters, whilst cheery, were modest and beginning to look tatty in parts. What she wouldn't do to see the house as it used to be, tables in each room groaning under the weight of arrangements such as this.

Laurence *had* to pull this off. It was the only way they'd be able to save Almer Hall, to stave off the necessity of its sale. She couldn't see it pass into other hands. It would be the final straw for her parents, who had already lost so much.

She pinged her eyes open with a swirling sense of discontent, but when her eyes naturally landed in the mirror above the flowers her gaze connected sharply with a pair of eyes that had been fascinating her all evening, and they were watching her with undisguised speculation. Her breath began to clog in her throat, making her feel light-headed.

'Did you get lost?' A sardonic lift of one brow was accompanied by a smile that set off a sudden round of fireworks in her belly. The desire she'd been trying so hard to fight lurched through her anew.

She shook her head, her throat parched at this man's sudden appearance. Even more so when his eyes lowered, carrying out a visual inspection of her body in the pale-grey silk slip she wore.

Her heart in her throat, she turned to face him, the action bringing them toe to toe.

'You're shorter than I would have thought,' he murmured so that it was Jemima's turn to lift her brows in silent enquiry. 'Most of the models I know are closer to my height.'

'And I suppose you know lots of models?' The words emerged husky and soft, and for some reason she didn't step back from him, even when it would have made sense to put a little distance between them.

'A few,' he confirmed in a way that made her certain he was intentionally under-stating the facts. But then his expression sobered and he was looking at her more intently, concentrating on her features as though committing them to memory. 'You are tiny. Like a little bird.'

Her lop-sided smile was spontaneous. 'I don't think anyone's ever called me that before.'

He continued to stare at her and her smile dropped. She was conscious of everything: the feeling of her breath in her body, the sound of his, the warmth from his chest, the parting of his lips.

'Anyway.' She shifted her eyes towards the door with effort. 'Laurence will be wondering what's keeping me.'

Cesare's expression shifted immediately. 'On the contrary, I think it is fair to say his entire focus is on whether or not I'm going to save his ass from financial ruin.'

At that, Jemima's gaze skittered back to Cesare. No one knew about Laurence's situation. He'd taken great care to hide the parlous state of the fund, particularly given the risky investments he'd been making with other people's capital. She tried not to think about the fact that he'd drawn her into this mess, nor to wonder whether that made her some kind of accessory. No one was supposed to know. Surely this man, this fascinating, handsome hunk of an Italian tycoon, couldn't really have any idea as to the full extent of Laurence's situation?

'You're surprised?' He correctly interpreted the look flitting across her expressive face. Her skin paled, her lips parted, and she stayed resolutely silent—for lack of any certainty about just what to say.

His body shifted, moving ever so slightly closer to hers—by only a matter of degrees, but it was enough. Enough for everything about him to become bigger, stronger and more overpowering and for all the temptations she'd been fighting off to threaten to consume her. 'Do I strike you as a man who would come to a meeting like this—or to any meeting, for that matter—unprepared?'

'No.' The answer was intuitive.

Approval warmed his face and he nodded, just once, not moving his eyes from her face. 'So you're, what—bait?'

She frowned, not understanding.

'Did Laurence think that having you at the table would distract me sufficiently to make me rush into this investment? That I'd put aside common sense and offer to buy into his hedge fund to the tune of half a billion pounds just because the most beautiful woman I've ever seen happened to be fluttering her lashes at me all evening?'

It wasn't really a compliment, yet butterflies beat their wings against the sides of her belly. There was an insult in there, or at the very least the hint of condemnation. A need to defend her cousin stiffened her spine. 'On the contrary, Laurence simply wanted it to feel like a pleasant evening rather than purely business.'

Cesare's wolf-like smile showed how little he believed that statement. 'This is business.' He growled the words out. 'And I never let anything affect my judgement where business is concerned.' He moved closer, so now his arm brushed against hers, and she had to suck in a sharp breath of air—which was a mistake, because it tasted of him, all hyper-masculine and citrusy.

'Although, you have made that hard to re-member at times.'

Another compliment buried in a tone that was somehow derisive. She stared up at him, the pale overhead light catching her hair so it shone like threads of precious gold. 'Have I?'

His expression was droll. 'As I'm sure you're aware.' He lifted a hand, running a finger across her cheek, and she trembled in response. 'It was an excellent gambit.' His thumb padded across her lower lip and desire sparked like flames against her sides. 'I can see why he would think you might win me over.'

'That wasn't his intention.' Her voice came out stiff and cultured, her tone plummy enough to please even her mother.

Cesare's laugh spread through her veins like warmed caramel. 'Yes, it was. Perhaps he didn't inform you of that, but I have no doubt your cousin believed that serving you up on a silver platter would make this deal go through more smoothly.'

'I'm not being served up, to you or anyone,' she demurred without moving backwards, even when she knew she had to. 'I often accompany Laurence on business meetings.' It wasn't particularly convincing.

'Really?' He lowered his hand to her shoulder, his eyes chasing the gesture, fixating on the exposed flesh there, pale cream with a pearl-like translucence.

'You find that hard to believe?'

'Yes.'

'Why?'

'Because it's hardly your scene, is it?'

'My scene?' Her heart threw an extra beat into its rhythm.

'International supermodel attends dinner meeting regarding finance fund?'

His mockery made her pulse skitter. 'You think the two are mutually exclusive, Mr Durante?'

'Call me Cesare.'

She found she couldn't resist. 'Cesare.' His name in her mouth was erotic. She pronounced it as he had, 'Che-zar-eh', then swallowed, trying to quell the buzzing that was spreading through her. 'It doesn't matter what I call you. It doesn't change the fact that your opinion is pretty offensive.'

'Name three of the companies your cousin has stakes in.'

She blinked.

'Any three. There are twenty-seven in the hedge fund.'

Heat bloomed in her cheeks. 'I'm not interested in the details.'

'No, you're not. And you're not here to talk business.'

'You honestly think I'm here as some kind of inducement to you?'

He shrugged. 'I cannot fathom any other reason for your presence.'

She glared at him, shaking her head. 'Yeah, well, you're wrong...'

'I doubt that.' His eyes bore into hers and then swept her face. 'You know, I've seen your photo dozens of times. You're everywhere— on buses, billboards, television. You are beautiful always, but in person you are much more so.' He frowned, as though he hadn't intended this to be a compliment. 'If Laurence thought

I would lose my mind and simply agree to sign on the bottom line, then he played an excellent bargaining chip.' He dropped his head lower so his lips were only inches from hers. 'I suspect one night with you would be worth half a billion pounds.'

Desire was like a tidal wave crashing over her.

'You don't know anything about me,' she murmured, but didn't move away.

His lips twisted cynically. 'I know what the rumours say. I know that you and Clive Angmore had an affair that almost ended his marriage, despite the fact he was in his sixties and you were barely legal.'

Her heart strangled at that familiar accusation. It was surprising how much it hurt coming from Cesare. After all, she'd lived alongside Clive's lies for a long time—she'd thought she'd developed a thicker skin than this. But hearing Cesare shame her for the supposed affair cut her to the quick.

'And you blame me for that?'

'No.' His eyes were thoughtful. 'As I said, you were just a teenager.'

If she'd been surprised by the hurt his accusation had caused then his next statement was a balm she also hadn't expected. 'Surely you're too intelligent to believe everything you read in the paper?'

'Not everything,' he murmured, the words drugging her with their sensual tone. 'But I've also observed that the old adage "where there's smoke, there's fire" is often true.'

She compressed her lips. It bothered her so much that he had clearly bought into all the rumours, was so believing of the image that the press had created of her 'out of control' lifestyle.

'You're wrong, Mr Durante.' She deliberately reverted to the use of his formal name. 'I'm here to support my cousin, and nothing more.' Her voice wobbled a little, but she was pleased with the coldness of her tone. And now, finally, she side-stepped him, gratefully breathing in Durante-free air.

No, not gratefully. Wistfully. She would have been grateful if she'd stayed exactly where she was, because in a matter of seconds she suspected he'd have been kissing her.

Her mind splintered apart at the very idea and a rush of warmth pooled low in her abdomen.

'Stop.' She couldn't say why she obeyed, but her legs remained perfectly still, unmoving, her face tilted towards his. He was watching her carefully, as though he could peel away her layers and see something deep inside.

'I came here tonight with a sense of amusement. I am not a man to be baited by a beautiful woman. And yet...' He lifted his hand to her cheek once more, his eyes roaming her face thoughtfully.

'And yet?' Her voice was croaky.

'I'd be lying if I said I wasn't tempted.' He didn't move but she felt as though his body was touching her, pressing into her, and her stomach twisted into a billion knots.

'I'm not bait,' she insisted. If only he knew that her experience with the opposite sex was completely non-existent.

He brushed aside her words with a flash of his eyes. 'I want you to come home with me tonight.' Before she could say anything in response, he lifted a finger and pressed it to her lips. 'It will have no bearing on my decision with the hedge fund. Business is business.'

He paused, his eyes devouring her inch by inch. 'Pleasure is pleasure.'

His finger against her lips moved to outline her Cupid's bow. 'Come home with me because you feel what I feel. Come home with me because you're as fascinated by this as I am.' He leaned closer so his warm breath buzzed her temple. 'Come home with me because you want me to make love to you all night long, until your body is exhausted and your voice hoarse from crying my name over and over again.'

She sucked in a sharp breath. Words were beyond her.

'Come home with me, Jemima.'

Her knees were weak, her pulse insistent. She swallowed but her throat felt thick; everything was out of whack.

She couldn't seriously be considering this. Cesare Durante was a renowned bachelor, a self-made billionaire who had no time for relationships that lasted more than a few days. She hadn't needed to run his name through an Internet search to know that—it was an established fact. He wasn't offering anything except one night—sex.

He obviously bought into the articles in the press, the ones that made it look as if she spent her life getting hammered at parties and sleeping with any guy that moved. She'd lost track of how many fictional relationships she'd been in, secret marriages she'd walked out of, how many times she'd been pregnant, dumped and broken-hearted. How many times in rehab, fighting with other models, all of it preposterous and laughable—except she didn't often laugh about it. She simply didn't read the stories any more.

Her manager had hired an exceptional public relations guru who only contacted Jemima when a story wouldn't die, something Jemima was required to respond to, but otherwise Jemima let the papers run their fictional pieces while she got on with her real life. And that was about as far removed from the public's perception as it was possible to get. She spent more time with her hands wrangling tulip bulbs than they did any man.

He had the wrong idea about her. He'd be disappointed if he learned she had precisely zero experience in bed. And she didn't want him to be disappointed in her.

'I can't.' Her reluctance wasn't faked.

'You don't want to?' he murmured, and now his lips brushed hers so her knees felt as though they were going to collapse beneath her. A soft moan escaped without her intention.

But she did. She wanted to go home with him in a way that should have served as a warning. Her hand lifted of its own accord to wrap around his neck, drawing his head lower, her eyes hitched to his. 'I don't even know you,' she pointed out, but the words were so quiet she might as well not have spoken.

'You know it would be good,' he replied simply, and she nodded, because she did. But he had no idea—he couldn't know what he was getting.

This was crazy. It was utterly mad, yet she felt something inside her tip, and all she could think of was how badly she wanted to do this.

It wasn't as though she'd planned to remain a virgin. Saying no had become a habit, one she was glad of. She'd seen more than her fair share of heartbreak and hurt amongst the models she worked with, models who slept with photographers only to discover the photographer was married, or sleeping with half a dozen other models.

But Cesare was different. He wasn't in the fashion industry at all; they'd never have to see each other again. She could sleep with him, lose her virginity, discover a little bit about the whole sex thing and then get on with her life. Truth be told, she was reaching a point where she felt that her virginity required an explanation and it would be nice not to think about that. Yes, it was a burden, and she'd be glad to be rid of it. And at least with Cesare she could be assured of two things: it would be meaningless and it would be good…

There were a thousand reasons not to do this, but none of them as drugging as the reasons to say yes. Even before she'd come face to face with him, she'd been fascinated by the legend of Cesare Durante, curious about the man who, as the stories said, had gone from being the dirt-poor son of an Italian nanny to one of the richest men in the world. He had the Midas touch, and his confidence was its own source of power and attractiveness. But, now that she'd met him, there was so much more to Cesare, so much more that had caught her completely in his thrall, so she found herself nodding slowly, almost without her knowledge.

'It has nothing do with Laurence.'

His smile was lightly mocking and, damn it,

even that she found sexier than she should have. 'I would hope not.' He leaned a little closer. 'I can assure you, he will be the furthest thing from your mind when I make you mine.'

A frown formed on her features, disbelief and uncertainty being swallowed up by a fierce rush of desire. *Make you mine.* The words held such a promise of possession and intent that she was already craving him, craving this. Tonight would be the night she lost her virginity and, all of a sudden, she could barely wait.

'I will make you sing, little bird.' He murmured the words against her ear, so goose bumps spread across her body. 'Come home with me.'

Common sense was completely submerged by desire, so she nodded, her hooded eyes finding his a second before his lips crushed hers. 'Yes,' she agreed into his mouth, though the word was barely necessary. Her hands wrapped around his neck, her body arching to press to his, her agreement evident in every cell of her body. Still, she said it again, partly to convince herself this made sense and also to reassure herself this was really happening. 'Yes, Cesare. Yes.'

He lifted his head to stare down into her eyes. 'Words I am going to make you scream soon.' The grey of his eyes flashed with a silent promise. Her nipples tightened against the soft fabric of her dress and, when he stepped back, his attention dropped to the tell-tale sign of arousal so that heat flashed in her face. 'You are going to be begging me to take you, and I am going to enjoy that.'

CHAPTER TWO

CESARE EYED THE beautiful model across the table, a tightness in his body that came from the pleasurable spread of anticipation—the certainty that enjoyment was near at hand.

He threw back a measure of the scotch, relishing the depth of its flavour, the aged quality that was full of spice. Cesare liked a good scotch—the finest. There were many things he could do without, many luxuries he could afford but rarely indulged in, because he'd spent much of his life doing without, sacrificing.

But now he liked nice things, he liked them when he wanted them. Scotch. A great meal with a world-class view. Being able to get in his jet and fly wherever he wanted on a whim. And women. He liked women who were beautiful, interesting, experienced and sophisticated. He liked sex without strings, without complications, sex that could entertain him and satisfy him without requiring him to think about a woman once he'd left her bed.

Jemima Woodcroft was undoubtedly all these things and he relished the chance to get to know her body, to pleasure her and delight in her before relegating her to the back of his mind, as he always did with women with whom he spent a night.

His mind ran at its usual frenetic pace as he analysed the deal Laurence was desperately laying before him, but he was conscious of every single movement Jemima made, every shift of her body, flutter of her eyelids, purse of her lips.

Despite the disastrous state of Laurence's hedge fund, Cesare could see the value in the offering. There was a lot of chaff, but a few of the investments packaged in with the group were substantial. One in particular stood on the brink of making major market inroads, and there was value in that, value in investing at ground level. It was clear that Laurence didn't understand what cards he held, or he would be shopping around instead of targeting one investor. If Cesare bailed, Laurence would be sunk.

Good. Nothing suited Cesare better than a

desperate negotiator. Desperation made people stupid.

Cesare attributed his success in business to three factors. First, he left nothing to chance. He researched his business options aggressively, arming himself with every bit of information he could. Second, he was hungry in a way no amount of wealth could ever remove. Poverty as a child—so spectacularly in contrast to the extreme wealth that had surrounded him at the grand country houses in which his mother had worked—had left Cesare with a feeling that a blazing fire was always right at his heels, chasing him through life in a way that would never ease. True, it had turned him into a workaholic, but he didn't see any problem with that. Finally, he obeyed his instincts as though his life depended on them.

His instincts told him Jemima was going to be a fantastic lover; he was relishing the prospect of taking her to his bed, despite the fact he usually gave aristocrats a wide enough berth that he could land on the moon.

Still, there was something about her, and it had nothing to do with her cousin's predicament.

Cesare's instincts also told him Laurence was

beyond desperate. He could smell the panic in the other man, feel it in his every frantic gesture, in the frequent glances he was shooting Jemima's way, as though half-expecting her to intervene, to say something to help him.

Jemima, though, was silent. Cesare couldn't have said how she was feeling, or if she was regretting her earlier agreement. She was one of the few people he'd met in his life that he found difficult to read. Her body language was relaxed enough. She was leaning back in her chair, champagne glass resting loosely between her fingertips—the same glass she'd been sitting on all evening—her eyes following Laurence and then Cesare without making any attempt to join in their conversations.

Knowing what was coming next, he was more than ready to put an end to this portion of the night. 'Fine.' He nodded, regarding Laurence carefully. 'You have my interest.'

'Your interest?'

Cesare had to bite back a smile when he saw how crestfallen the British man was. The only reason he didn't give vent to his amusement was that Jemima was watching him. He could feel her gaze on his face, and was well aware that she wouldn't take kindly to him ridiculing Laurence's expectations. Besides, despite a life-long hatred for men like Laurence—spoiled, entitled British brats—there was something in Laurence that Cesare could almost have grudgingly come to like.

'You don't expect me to sign away five hundred million pounds on the spot, do you?'

'I just think it's a really rare opportunity,' Laurence muttered, dragging a hand through his hair. 'And you're getting first option.'

Cesare leaned forward. 'Let's not play with one another. I'm getting the only option.'

Laurence's face glowed pink. 'No, I happen to have a couple of very cashed-up investors on the hook.'

Now Jemima's head swivelled towards Laurence and for the first time in at least thirty minutes she slipped up. Cesare saw the consternation that crossed her features and he understood it. Underneath the table, Cesare lightly ran his fingers over her exposed knee, so now her face jerked back to his, her lips parted in that sensual way she had. His cock strained against his trousers. Anticipation drummed against the fabric of his soul.

'Sure you do.' Cesare's grin was tight. 'Then let me know what they bid and, if I decide I'm still interested, I'll better it.'

Backed into a corner, Laurence grimaced. 'You're my first choice. I know your history. Plus, an investment by you brings a hell of a lot of prestige. Everything you touch turns to gold.'

Cesare heard his words and wondered if he'd ever tire of this. Laurence was exactly the kind of preppy school boy who'd been intent on making Cesare's life hell for a time, and now he was begging for his kindness, his money, his grace. His chest felt three sizes bigger. He regarded the other man for several seconds, enjoying this experience way more than he should, and then pushed his chair back.

'I'll be in touch.'

Laurence stood a few seconds later. 'You will?'

Cesare dipped his head. 'Yes.'

'Okay.' Laurence was ambivalent. He turned to Jemima, who was still sitting down, lost in thought. Doubt briefly dimmed Cesare's sense of anticipation because a huge part of his present mood came down to the certainty he would soon be pleasuring this very beautiful woman from head to toe—and everywhere in between.

'Jemima?' he murmured, and she raised her eyes to his in consternation.

Laurence frowned. 'Jem?'

'I've offered your cousin a lift home,' Cesare inserted smoothly.

'Oh, but you don't have to do that.' Laurence frowned.

'It's been agreed.' Cesare's tone held warning, a warning any of his rivals would know to listen to. And Laurence heeded it now, choosing instead to address Jemima.

'Are you sure? It's no trouble for me to drop you off...'

Cesare was surprised to realise he was holding his breath, awaiting her reply. After what felt like several minutes, but was actually just a few seconds, she stood, placing her still half-full champagne flute on the table.

'No, really, it's fine.' She eyed Cesare, something strange in her expression—trepidation or uncertainty, something he couldn't quite make sense of. But then she smiled and her whole face lit up, as though an army of firebugs had filled her blood. She glowed from the inside out, and his gut kicked with an unmistakable rush of sensual heat. 'I'm ready to go.'

In the restaurant, he'd been an impressive specimen, but here in the confines of his luxury car Cesare Durante was like a whole other species. This was madness but she couldn't summon even an inch of hesitation.

It was one of the pitfalls of her job that she was expected to attend events and parties, and it seemed to go hand in hand with her attendance that she was there to hook up. But she never had. Somehow, seeing such overt sexuality on display had inured her to its effects. Curiosity had been subverted by something approaching prudishness and then, as the years had gone by, embarrassment. Embarrassment about her virginity and what people would say if they knew the truth. And here she was, in the car with a man she found unbearably sexy, and some time tonight she'd lose her innocence... She couldn't wait.

A hint of anxiety creased through her for a moment when she thought of Laurence. Was there any chance being with Cesare could negatively impact the likelihood of Cesare investing in Laurence's fund? Surely not? He'd said as much, hadn't he? Business was business, distinct from pleasure.

She shifted her gaze sideways, eyeing him thoughtfully. He was immaculately dressed. His suit, a charcoal grey, contrasted perfectly with his crisp white shirt, and his black shoes were polished to gleaming. His hair was neat, his nails too. His fingers were long and capable-looking, with hair-roughened knuckles.

They didn't speak in the car. It was as though neither of them could find words, or perhaps both were equally afraid that talking would cut through the spell that had weaved some kind of magic around them, binding them together in a shared moment of madness.

London zipped past, all bright lights and ancient buildings, and then the car was running alongside Hyde Park, bringing them into Knightsbridge. It pulled off the road at a large and gracious townhouse. Despite the age of the building, modern modifications had taken place and an underground garage had been installed.

The car slid into it effortlessly, a gate closing behind them. Only then did Cesare turn to her, speculation in his face, as though waiting for her to change her mind.

She didn't want to.

It was insanity, but it was also the thing she wanted most in the world.

At his look of enquiry, she smiled. 'What are we waiting for?'

He expelled a breath and leaned forward, his lips claiming hers quickly, tasting her so she moaned, lifting her hands to the lapels of his shirt and gripping him tightly.

'Not a goddamned thing. Come on.' He growled the instructions into her mouth then pushed his door open, holding it and waiting for her to step out. She'd entered and exited limousines with the world's press waiting to get a shot up her skirt. She knew precisely how to disembark with an air of dignity—but it was a lot trickier to manage when her knees were quivering and warmth was spreading through her in anticipation of what was to come.

Despite the fact this was a residential address, there was a lift on the other side of the basement. He laced his fingers through hers, pulling her towards it, his enthusiasm making her smile even as his face was so serious.

The lift was as elegant as you'd see in any five-star hotel. More so, in fact, because it had only one occupant, so there was no wear and tear, no scruffy carpet. It was immaculate, just like Cesare—highly polished wood-panelling, a darkly tinted mirror and five buttons, indicating it served the whole house.

'Five storeys?'

His eyes pinned her to the spot. 'A basement and a rooftop terrace,' he pointed out. 'So only three.'

'Oh, that's far more modest.'

His expression showed scepticism as the lift doors opened onto the second floor. He held the door open, waiting for her to step out. 'And you live in a flat share, I suppose?' he responded.

'I live in a flat.' She shrugged. 'Nothing like this.' She waved her hand around the room. The lights had come on when they'd stepped out of the lift, subdued and golden, and they filled the space with a warmth its furnishings required. It was…austere. Yes, that was probably the best way to describe it. She looked around and, even as she recognised every piece was the very best, designer and in brand-new condition, there was an incredible lack of personality.

'Do you spend much time here?' she asked, genuinely curious. After all, it didn't exactly look lived in.

'No.'

'Ah.' She was strangely pleased by that. It wasn't even remotely homely.

'This is good?' he prompted. 'Are you worried I'm going to want to see you again after tonight?'

She stilled, her eyes finding his. That thought hadn't even occurred to her. In fact, she hadn't spent any time thinking about what happened later, tomorrow. 'I...'

'Relax, *uccellina*.' He said the word in his native tongue, and she had no idea what it meant. 'This is strictly a one-night thing.'

Her eyes flared wide, her heart lurching at the line he was drawing. She was glad—simple, quick, no complications. That was better for everyone, including Laurence. 'Perfect,' she murmured, her pulse slamming through her veins.

'I wanted you the moment I saw you tonight.' Something like determination glowed ferociously in his eyes and, for no reason she could think of, a frisson of something like a warning shifted down her spine.

'And here I am.' There was fatalism in her words.

He didn't react.

'Why do I think you always get exactly what you want?'

'What do you base that on?' His hand lifted to the flimsy strap of her dress, sliding beneath it, running it down her shoulder slowly, his eyes holding hers.

'Am I wrong?'

His eyes flared. 'No, *uccellina*.' His fingers ran lower, tracing her arm lightly, his gaze not shifting.

It was the second time he'd used that word. 'What does that mean?'

His hand moved to the other strap, gliding it over her flesh so her breath snagged in her throat.

'Little bird.' His words were gravelled. The straps slipped lower until the dress began to fall. She bit down on her lower lip to stop a sigh escaping. The fabric was silk, and it moved like water over her breasts, her nipples puckering at the slight touch. His hands guided the dress lower still, over her hips, until it fell to the floor, leaving her standing in front of him in only a pair of heels and a lace thong.

Her breathing was ragged, her body covered in goose bumps that had nothing to do with the temperature.

'You are beautiful,' he murmured seriously, the words factual rather than said as a compliment. 'But this you already know.'

It was a statement that came close to implying she was vain, and Jemima resented it, but before she could respond he'd stepped closer so that his body was hard against hers and urgency made it difficult to think, much less speak. She could feel every inch of him, every expansive muscle, his arousal pressed to her belly.

Her hands lifted to his chest, pushing against his shirt, his pectoral muscles firm beneath her curious grip. She undid his buttons one by one, starting at his neck and working down, pausing at the waistband of his trousers so she could lift his shirt out completely. The tip of her tongue darted from the corner of her lips as she concentrated on what she was doing, but before she could push the shirt from his body he'd swooped his head down and sought her mouth with his, his lips mashing to hers, the kiss driven by a mutual, desperate passion.

He took another step forward, so her back connected with the glass window, and he rolled his hips, leaving her in little doubt as to how much he wanted her.

Lust was a new feeling for Jemima. Never had she felt so attracted to a man that she wanted to act on it like this. Her brain had ceased to function; she was operating purely on instinct and her instincts were telling her to enjoy this.

'I need to...' What? See him? Touch him? Feel him? Frustrated by her lack of experience, her total inability to put into words what she was feeling and to explain the fever in her blood, she shook her head.

But he understood, of course he did, because the same fever was raging through him. He scooped her up, wrapping her legs around his waist, carrying her easily through the house, kissing her the entire way, and by the time they reached a bedroom and he dropped her onto the mattress she was ready to catch fire completely.

'I want...'

'Yes?' His own voice was roughened by desire. 'What do you want, Jemima?'

There it was again—the mental block, a complete inability to say what she was thinking. She groaned, reaching for him, sitting up and pulling at his sides, but he didn't move. He kicked out of his shoes, watching her, his chest rising and falling with each of his deep breaths as he shrugged out of his shirt.

He had a tattoo that ran just beneath his heart: *'come sono'*. Her Italian was limited to industry terms and social niceties. '"I am me"?' she said aloud, her eyes chasing the cursive ink.

'"As I am".' He stepped out of his trousers and now a kick of fear hit her gut. Not fear of what was to come, but fear at how out of her depth she was. Her pulse lurched wildly through her body and she knew she should say something. But ancient feminine instincts gave her confidence and had her pushing to the end of the bed so that his legs straddled hers, his body so big, his presence overpowering. His fingers curved through her hair, and then her lips sought his flat chest, pressing to the ridges there as she scrambled onto her knees on the edge of the bed so she could trace one of his nipples with her tongue, flicking it curiously before transferring her attention to the next one.

In the back of her mind, she was vaguely aware of how new this was, and yet she didn't feel anything except pleasurable anticipation and relief. She wanted this. She wanted it so badly. Soon, her virginity would be gone, and she'd know the pleasure of a man's body... She couldn't wait.

His chest moved rapidly with each curious little exploration of her tongue. Power trilled in her veins—the knowledge that she was driving him as wild as she was set her pulse skittering.

CHAPTER THREE

OVER DINNER SHE'D admired the strength of his arms but now, without a shirt, she saw for herself that he was muscled in a way that suggested he worked out often. There was a sense of power and control in his every movement. His chest was ridged with muscles and his flesh showed a deep tan, as though he spent a lot of time outdoors.

He reached down, his fingers tangling in the elastic of her thong, sliding the underwear over her legs in a way that was so sensual and tantalising she couldn't bear it. She ached to reach down and remove it herself to speed this up not because she wanted it to end—she already knew she didn't—but because she needed it to begin. She needed him as though he were oxygen.

His mouth on her breast was completely unexpected. His tongue curled around her nipple, perhaps retaliating for her own leisurely exploration. But his was so much more skilled, so much more thorough. It wasn't a fair match at all.

His tongue swirled around the dusky peach areola and then he drew it into his mouth, sucking there until she was moaning, moist heat slicked between her legs. His other hand curved around her breast so his fingers could torment that nipple, alternating between a light, barely there brush of his fingers to a tight squeeze that sent arrows of desire firing against her flesh.

'Please,' she moaned, no longer aware what she was asking for, knowing only that she needed something he alone could provide. He was still wearing boxer shorts but he pressed his arousal to her womanhood and she writhed at the pressure, the unexpected intimacy of that gesture. His body thrust against hers as though they were already making love, and she ached to be. She ached to feel him inside her.

She'd always wondered if it would hurt— losing her virginity—but in this moment she was far too caught up in the hedonism of sensation to anticipate anything other than wild, utter bliss.

Her nails dug into his shoulders and her lips

kept searching for his. His kiss was a temporary balm to the wildness in her veins but not
enough—there would never be enough. She
needed complete surrender—his? Hers? She
didn't know.

'I need you,' she groaned, her hands moving down his back, her nails scraping against
his flesh and pushing into the waistband of his
shorts so she could curve her grip around his
buttocks and hold him tight to her sex. She
lifted her hips wordlessly, instinctively invit-
ing him to sweep away her invisible barrier, to
become one with her.

'I wanted to do this the moment I saw you,'
he muttered, moving to stand, pushing at his
boxers impatiently. His eyes were fixed to her
face with something like impatience—or possibly accusation—something she didn't understand and couldn't fathom. He reached to his
side, pulling a condom from the bedside table,
watching her as he opened the foil square.

She stared at him, transfixed, as he rolled it
over the length of his cock, so big and hard,
so fascinating. Her throat was dry, her heart
pounding, and for the first time since agreeing
to this she felt doubts creep in.

Not doubts about wanting him.

Doubts about the fact he didn't know about her inexperience.

She didn't need to be a mind-reader to recognise that Cesare Durante was a man who was used to sophisticated lovers. She was pretty sure springing her virginity on him would be poor form.

Her cheeks warmed now with the beginnings of embarrassment rather than desire, and she pushed up to stare at him, disbelief that her conscience was getting the better of her making her frown.

'I am going to make you scream my name,' he murmured, oblivious to the direction of her thoughts. 'Over and over and over again.'

She nodded, but when he brought his body over hers she lifted a hand and pressed it to his chest. Their heads were level, his steel-grey eyes boring into hers, and Jemima told herself to have courage—to do the right thing. It wasn't that big a deal, she reasoned. Surely he wouldn't really care?

'I have to tell you something.' She swallowed, her pupils huge in her pale eyes.

'Tell me quickly.' He brought his mouth

to her cheek, kissing her there, dragging his tongue down her body to the valley between her breasts and lower, over her flat stomach towards her womanhood. Of their own accord her hands tangled in his hair, pulling at it frantically. When his mouth connected with her feminine core, she startled, pushing up on her elbows, uncertainty losing the battle to pleasure.

His tongue ran along her seam and she twisted on the bed in an instinctive response so that his hands gripped her thighs and moved her legs wider, clamping down on them and holding her right as he wanted her.

His name tumbled from her lips, just as he'd said it would, the Italian word so exotic in her mouth, so moreish and tempting. Pleasure was a wave building within her and she couldn't stay afloat. It sucked her down into a turbulent ocean and she didn't even care that she was drowning. She didn't care that she could barely breathe.

Her fingers tousled his hair, pulling at it frantically as pleasure eroded her awareness of time and place, and finally she exploded, breaking free of the ocean and finding her place amongst the stars. The orgasm claimed her, every cell of her, every fibre of her being. She was celestial matter, she was time and place, she was ancient and new, she was indefinable.

Pleasure was a thousand barbs beneath her skin. She lay back against the bed, her breathing rushed, her sanity in tatters. His body was coming over her, so even as she was ship-wrecked on the shore line of their passion she knew she had to find a way to speak and be heard.

'Cesare, wait.' The urgency of her words stalled him. He braced his body over hers and she felt his sheathed arousal at the entrance to her womanhood; she was so hungry for him and more of this that for a brief second she contemplated not speaking. 'You have to know...'

'Yes?' His tip nudged at her entrance and she groaned, pressing her hands to his chest, wanting him with a ferocity that was beyond her comprehension.

'I want you. I really, really want this.' The words were breathless. She looked up at him and said nothing else. She wasn't sure why— she knew telling him of her innocence was the *right* thing to do—but when she opened her mouth she simply couldn't find the words. Instead, she heard the cacophony of news articles about her, the names she'd been called, the marriages she was said to have ruined, and she was struck dumb, silent in the face of the world's assumptions.

He stared down at her, his gaze intent enough to see all the way into her soul, and then he smiled, a look of such complete confidence and sexy dominance that her heart exploded, taking up all the space that should have been reserved for her lungs, making breathing impossible.

'I want you.' It was the last thing she said before he thrust into her, claiming her and removing her innocence in one hard movement.

Cesare froze, holding his body where it was with the greatest of efforts, his arousal buried inside the beautiful Jemima as shock tore through him. He'd been a teenager the last time he'd slept with a virgin and it had been a disaster. A simple act of sex to Cesare had meant the world to her and, after seeing the way he'd carelessly broken her heart, he'd sworn he'd never again sleep with an innocent woman.

And he hadn't. He'd steered clear of anyone

sexually inexperienced because there was a burden in being a woman's first.

Her tightness was unmistakable, as was the resistance he hadn't felt until he was already inside her, too late to change what had happened. He pushed up onto his elbows, his breathing ragged, and even as question after question spilled through him her muscles squeezed him, filling his eyes with white light, blinding him with his own insatiable need for release.

'Damn it.' The words were clipped, gruff.

'Don't.' The wobble in her voice had him refocussing his gaze on her. 'Don't stop. Please.' His eyes chased her features: the tell-tale flush of pink running towards her brow, lips that were swollen from how she'd been biting down on them, pupils that filled her irises almost completely. 'Please.'

He swore softly because he suspected wild horses couldn't have forced him to stop, even as he knew he would have if she'd been in pain. He moved his body more gently, though, slowly allowing her time to adjust to the feeling of his possession, to acclimatise to the sense of having him inside her, watching her carefully for every flicker of response that crossed her face.

Emotions he hadn't expected pounded him—and emotions were something he generally preferred to keep way, way out of his sex life. But, for the first time in a long time, he felt a heavy sense of guilt. Of responsibility—a feeling of having done something wrong.

'Oh, God, Cesare...'

The sound of his name on her perfectly shaped lips dragged him back to the present, to the physical and the pressing, the passion and the perfection of this. Her nails on his back were desperate, as though she could scratch past pleasure and bring herself back to sanity. There was only one way for that—and he needed the release as badly as she did.

He might have teased her and tormented her, drawing out her orgasm, withholding the ultimate pleasure until she was almost incandescent with desire, tormenting her with the strength of her longing. He would have done so if this had been any ordinary night, any ordinary lover.

But that was gamesmanship and he didn't feel like playing games any more.

Her cries became fevered, her body writhing as pleasure threatened to tear her apart, and when she tipped over the edge he followed her, releasing himself without making a sound, already mentally detaching himself from this, from her, even as he tipped himself inside her and felt her muscles spasm wildly around his length.

This had been a mistake—and Cesare Durante didn't make mistakes.

Nor was he a man who tolerated surprises. He stared down at the woman beneath him, her eyes fluttered shut, her breathing rapid, and he pulled away from her, removing himself, standing without saying a word. He couldn't.

He'd learned a long time ago not to react when he was angry, not to react when his emotions were in play, but in that moment he felt an odd fury, a sense of having been duped into something he would *never* knowingly have consented to. She'd been a virgin, and he hadn't offered anything beyond one night. What the actual hell?

When he'd been nine years old, a teacher had introduced him to a Rubik's Cube for the first time. It had been a simple warm-up exercise for the class, but Cesare hadn't been able to comprehend how inanimate plastic could not be bent to his will. He'd spent hours staring at it, moving each tile, until some time around midnight on that same day he'd brought order to the madness of the cube.

He felt that same desperate sense of misunderstanding now. Jemima Woodcraft—a virgin? Impossible. Except it wasn't. He'd felt the proof of her innocence for himself. He strode towards his en suite bathroom, dispensing with the proof of their love-making in the wastepaper basket, and with the same motion he grabbed a towel and wrapped it low around his waist.

He met the reflection of his eyes in the mirror, his expression grim. She'd come to his bed knowing what that would entail. Which left one question. Why the hell had she chosen to lose her virginity to him?

Calmer, he turned, moving back into his bedroom. She was sitting up, a sheet wrapped around her body, her gaze averted from his in a way that was infuriating and somehow endearing all at once.

'You were a virgin?' He didn't need the confirmation, yet it still seemed important to establish the fact beyond any doubt. Or perhaps he simply wanted to hear her admit it.

He clamped his jaw together and expelled a harsh breath so his nostrils flared. 'Jemima?'

His eyes narrowed, studying the pallor of her face, and frustration bit at his insides. She wouldn't look at him.

'Yes.' The word was soft.

'And you came here tonight to sleep with me?'

Now her face lifted, though she focussed her gaze about an inch above his shoulder. 'Yes.'

At least she wasn't lying to him. 'You didn't think this was something I ought to have known? Something I might have liked to consider?'

Her chin tilted at a defiant angle. 'I tried to tell you.'

Cesare frowned, guilt and disbelief churning in his gut. 'When?'

'Before! Before you—before we—before we were together,' she finished with a shake of her head. 'I tried but I...was embarrassed, I guess.'

'You thought it was better for me to feel your innocence as I obliterated it?'

She winced, her expression showing hurt.

'I don't know.'

For some reason, everything she said somehow made it worse. He felt angry. Disempowered. As though she'd taken what was supposed to be an easy exchange between two consenting lovers and turned it into something so much more complicated.

'You don't think this is something I deserved to know? To decide if I even wanted to be your first lover?'

Her face drained of colour. 'Would it have made a difference?'

He swore in his native tongue, the curse a harsh invective that slammed around the room and seemingly electrocuted her. She jack-knifed from the bed, the towel locked toga-style to her body.

But he didn't stop; he couldn't. 'You're damned right it would have made a difference. I don't *do* virgins, Jemima. What did you think? This would make me want to buy into your cousin's hedge fund? That I'd feel so guilty at having unknowingly become your first lover I'd pay whatever I could to absolve myself of that responsibility?'

She sucked in a sharp breath, her eyes narrowing. 'How dare you? This had *nothing* to do with Laurence.'

'I find that hard to believe.'

The column of her throat shifted as she swallowed. 'Be that as it may, it's the truth. I came here tonight because I wanted to sleep with you, not for any other reason.'

'And if I knew do you think I would still have wanted to sleep with you?'

Her cheeks paled and he told himself the sensation rolling through him was satisfaction.

'I honestly didn't think it would matter.'

'You were a twenty-three-year-old virgin. I brought you here thinking you were like me, that you enjoy sex for sport. If I had known you'd never been with another lover, I would never have touched you.'

She sucked in a breath that was pure indignation. 'Well, rest assured, Cesare, I have no intention of darkening your door ever again.' She glared at him, somehow managing to look elegant and haughty even as she crossed the room in a bed sheet.

But dissatisfaction rode through him. He still didn't have any of the answers he wanted. He followed her into the living room.

'How is this even possible? There are countless articles about your conquests online...'

'Yeah, and the Internet gets it wrong sometimes, you know.'

'But so completely wrong?'

She paused to shoot him a withering look. 'What do you think?'

Her dress had been discarded on the floor. She lifted it over her head and dislodged the sheet as she pulled it down so that he was deprived of another glimpse of her body. It didn't matter. The sight of her was likely burned into his memory anyway.

'There are photographs. And what about Clive Angmore?'

'An acquaintance,' she muttered, running her fingers through her hair as she looked around for her handbag. 'Nothing more.'

'So you were, what? Saving yourself for marriage?'

Her shocked gasp tumbled through the room and his heart twisted sharply in his chest. 'You should know, Jemima, that this makes no difference to me. For whatever reason you came here tonight, and whatever you were expecting it might mean to me, nothing has changed in my mind. This was just sex, nothing more.'

She glared at him, her expression pinched, her face wearing a mask of contempt, but the effect was lessened by eyes that were suspiciously shimmering, moisture dabbing her eyelashes. His gut rolled.

'I don't want anything from you.'

'So what? You intended for me, a man you barely know, to be your first lover? Why?'

'It's not like I had some elaborate plan,' she snapped. 'You asked me to come home with you and in that moment I couldn't think of a single reason not to.'

His eyes narrowed at the deceptive simplicity of her statement. 'I can give you a reason,' he said quietly. 'I had no interest in being your first. I didn't want the gift of your virginity. What we just did was a mistake.'

She blinked and a single tear threatened to fall from her eyes. He made a noise and turned away from her, his breathing uneven as he went behind the island bar of the kitchen.

He poured a scotch and when he looked up she was standing exactly where he'd left her, as though frozen in time.

Something shifted inside him. He hated that they'd slept together. All the feelings of panic he'd felt almost two decades ago came screeching back to him, but it was more than that. Cesare didn't like being surprised and she'd surprised him completely.

He hated that he'd completely misread her. He hated that she hadn't told him what he was getting into, and he hated looking at her now, knowing that the tear rolling lazily down her cheek was because of him. Most of all, he hated that he was awash with feelings because of her, when Cesare Durante was a man who prided himself on a robotic level of emotional detachment.

This whole night had been a complete mistake. When he spoke, it was with a stony cool.

'I'll have my driver take you home.'

Her eyes lifted to his face, a frown covering her lips. 'What?'

She looked completely lost. He swallowed past the unwelcome sense of compassion. 'My driver. He will take you home.'

She nodded then, and he felt as if she was going to say something. Then, she shook her head. 'Don't bother. I'll grab a cab.'

A thousand things ran through his mind. He should object. Tell her he wouldn't feel right not seeing her home, or knowing that she got there safely, say something to erase the lines of disbelief that had etched themselves on her brow.

It wasn't a question of caring, it was basic civility. 'Either my driver takes you home or I do. The choice is yours.'

She blanched visibly. 'Fine.' Her lips were a gash in her face. 'Call your driver, then. Frankly, I don't want to see you ever again.'

CHAPTER FOUR

Four weeks later

JEMIMA'S STOMACH ROLLED with a stormy kaleidoscope of butterflies. Anxiety burst through her, but even as the lift ascended to the top floor of Durante Incorporated's offices here in Rome and she gnawed on her lower lip, wondering if there was any alternative to this, she knew there wasn't.

She had to do this.

Her eyes, shielded by the over-sized sunglasses she often wore, flicked to the lift control panel. Buttons lit up as the lift crossed the floors until finally it arrived on the twenty-seventh. Jemima was pretty certain she'd left her stomach and every single one of her nerves down in the marbled lobby.

She'd dressed carefully for this meeting. Where she usually liked to fly under the radar, she felt she needed all her Jemima Woodcroft armour at her disposal today. Conversely, she hadn't wanted it to look as though she'd gone to any effort whatsoever. A pair of skinny jeans, a loose-fitting blouse a crisp white in colour, with a bright beaded necklace she'd bought at Camden Market and a pair of stilettos to give her a little extra height—and courage. Her clutch matched her necklace and she kept it tucked under her arm as she approached the central reception bay. Here, it was like another version of the lobby downstairs—all high ceilings, marble floor, bright and sun-filled, beautiful and extravagant. Everywhere she looked breathed 'success'.

'I'm here to see Cesare Durante.' His name flew from her lips and sparked a deluge of memories, the same memories that had been tormenting her night after night since she'd stalked out of his London home and sworn she'd never think of him again.

If only.

She had thought of him without meaning to. It had been hardest of all to keep him at bay when she'd been showering. Naked, her hands had run over her body, touching her flesh as he had, stirring memories and wants so that desire had begun to simmer inside her all the time. Anger was there too, anger at the way he'd reacted and treated her, but the pleasure of what they'd shared refused to be dimmed, regardless of what had come afterwards.

'Do you have an appointment?'

'No.' Jemima removed her sunglasses. 'But he'll want to see me. We're…old friends.'

The receptionist lifted her head belatedly, swiping at her silky black hair, pushing it back from her face. As her eyes landed on Jemima, she showed obvious surprise, and Jemima tamped down on a familiar feeling—part resentment, part amusement. It was easy to tell the moment people recognised her.

'Jemima Woodcroft?'

Jemima's smile was kind. 'Yes.'

'Oh, wow. Okay, I'll just let him know you're here.'

'Thank you.' She dipped her head forward in acknowledgement. A few moments later, moments in which Jemima's fingers fidgeted unstoppably, moments in which she began to imagine that perhaps he wasn't going to see her after all, the receptionist appeared at Jemima's side.

'This way, ma'am.'

Her feet made a clickety-clack noise as she crossed the reception area. When they approached two wide, glass doors, Jemima knew she was seconds away from seeing him again. Her insides were trembling; she employed every technique at her disposal, everything her professional training had taught her, to hide any outward appearance of nervousness. He couldn't know how he affected her, nor what this visit was costing her pride!

The receptionist opened the door and stood holding it. Jemima expelled a soft breath, dug her nails into her palms and pushed into his office.

And immediately wished she hadn't.

It was so, so very him. Dark timber floors, sleek and elegant, unbelievably masculine in its decor, and there was a faint hint of fragrance, something like pine needles and orange peel, that made her tummy loop around and around in circles with the rush of her memories.

Within seconds she'd taken in the details of the room, looking around on autopilot until her eyes landed on him with a heart-stopping thud and she had no scope left to notice anything else.

Oh, God.

A month. Four weeks. Thirty days. In that time she'd travelled to Istanbul for a magazine shoot, to Paris to film a video for an airline, but no matter where she'd fallen asleep, her dreams had been filled with Cesare, and her dreams were so torturously vivid that she'd woken up again and again and reached for him, as though her fingertips would connect with his warm, toned flesh.

She stared at him now as a drowning man might a lifeline. He wore a suit, dark blue with a tinge of grey, that set off the depth of his tan beautifully, teamed with a white shirt and a pair of brown shoes which she'd bet were hand-stitched. At his wrist there was a gold watch, and his dark hair was brushed back from his brow. He looked strong, vital and unbelievably sexy. She stared at him, wishing she'd pushed her glasses back onto her face, wishing she had some kind of shield, some sort of protection against this.

Images came to her unbidden. Memories of his mouth on her breasts, on her sex, of his tongue running over her body, tasting her, tormenting her, driving her completely wild. Her nerve endings began to tingle; she felt as though her feet had lifted up off the ground.

'Miss Woodcroft.' His use of her surname brought her to the present with a thud. She wasn't here to walk down memory lane— all ten yards of it. She was here on business. She was here for Laurence—that was the only reason she had for weakening and seeing him again. Memories of how desperate her cousin had been when they'd spoken on the phone two nights earlier surged through her now, making it easier to push past her anxiety and desire and focus almost exclusively on the purpose of her visit.

'Mr Durante,' she responded in kind, her eyes subconsciously icing over.

'Thank you, Olivia.'

The door clicked shut behind the receptionist, leaving them completely alone. Jemima was conscious of everything. Her breathing and his, the space between them, the rustle of his suit as he crossed the room to a kitchenette. He pressed a button on a machine and a thick, black liquid began to fill a white ceramic cup. 'Coffee?'

She shook her head, then cleared her throat. 'No, thank you. I'm fine.'

His eyes lifted to her face, scanning it thoughtfully, then he removed the cup from the machine and cradled it in his hand. 'Then perhaps you can explain what you're doing here?'

'Straight to it?' she murmured, as much for her own sake as his.

He sipped his coffee without speaking, his silence deeply unnerving.

She swallowed past her nerves, trying not to think of anything except her cousin. Nothing else mattered—he'd made that perfectly clear when he'd dismissed her from his house. 'I came to find out what's going on with the hedge fund.'

Cesare didn't visibly react, and the longer he stayed silent, the more anxious she became. The directness of his stare was completely unsettling. 'Laurence says you've had the contract a fortnight but you haven't been answering his calls.'

Cesare lifted his brows. 'And?'

Her stomach flipped and flopped. 'It's not

fair to keep him in suspense like this.' Her voice was crackly. She cleared her throat. 'If you're going to buy into the fund, you should do it. Otherwise tell him definitively so he can explore other options.'

Cesare's smile was wolf-like. 'Such as bankruptcy?'

Jemima felt the warmth fall from her face. It was a cruel thing to say and it showed in her features, hurt emanating from her as she spun away from him, moving towards the large boardroom that was framed by enormous glass windows.

'Either you're interested or not. Jerking him around like this...'

'He is asking for a large sum of money. You don't think some due diligence is required?'

Jemima placed her bag down on top of the table and focussed her gaze on the stunning vista of this ancient city. 'How long is that going to take?'

Silence. She was glad then that she wasn't looking at him. She felt his disapproval from a distance and she hated it.

'Let me get this straight,' he said finally. 'Laurence doesn't like how long I'm spending on this and so he sends you, knowing our history, in an attempt to motivate me?' He made a snorting noise of contempt. 'And you didn't think you'd try to guilt-trip me into anything?'

She sucked in a harsh breath, on the brink of denying his charge, but he continued before she could speak.

'I can see why he'd think I'd be persuaded, given what happened between us, but surely you've learned your lesson, Jemima? If you play with fire, you get burned, and I am definitely fire where you are concerned.'

She winced and spun around to find him closer now, only a few feet away, watching her with an intensity that made her heart skip a beat. 'He doesn't know I'm here,' she contradicted. 'And he doesn't know anything about that night. About what happened between us.'

She caught a flash of surprise in the depths of Cesare's eyes, but only briefly, and then he was cynical and detached once more.

'Then why are you here?' He prowled towards her, his eyes morphing from steel-grey to the colour of the ocean on a stormy day. Before she could realise his intention, he was right before her, his body so close they were brushing, his face intently watchful.

Her breath caught in her throat, and for a second she found it almost impossible to think, certainly to find any words to offer.

'I just think you should move faster.' She furrowed her brow. 'I'm *asking* you to make up your mind, one way or another. He deserves to know where he stands.'

Cesare's expression didn't shift. 'And you thought that if you came here to ask me to snap my fingers and invest in his fund I would simply agree?'

She shook her head. This was a mistake. Why had she thought he'd listen to her? Or that he'd have any motivation to help her?

'No. I guess I'm asking you as a decent human to put him out of his misery.' She swallowed. 'I know it's probably not good business sense to tell you how desperate he is but Cesare, truly, I'm worried about him.' She lowered her eyes so he wouldn't see how close she was to tears. 'He's at his wits' end. And he's worked too hard to lose everything now. He *can't* lose everything. Too much depends on it. Please.'

She'd said too much. This was a gamble she

was going to lose and the consequences would be disastrous. 'But you don't care, do you?' she whispered, wondering at the deep sense of surprise that permeated her.

'I barely know your cousin. If you're asking if I'm personally moved by your worries for him, then no. I told you that night, I do not mix business with pleasure. If you think that the fact we slept together somehow predisposes me to want to help Laurence, then you completely misunderstand the kind of man I am. He made his bed, and he may very well now have to lie in it.'

Panic scorched her, but she tried not to lose sight of the man Cesare was. No way would he have come to London to meet with Laurence if he hadn't been motivated to move. 'But you *are* interested in investing, right?'

He dipped his head forward in silent agreement.

'So why delay?'

Cesare's eyes sparked in his face. 'I'm not sure that's any business of yours.'

She bit down on her lip. He had a point.

This wasn't going to work. He was immovable. She should have known as much. All she'd succeeded in doing today was destroying her pride and possibly weakening Laurence's bargaining position in a way that may well prove fatal.

'You're right.' She shook her head. 'I shouldn't have come here. I really thought you might understand. I don't know why I should have expected anything of you, really. It was pretty obvious that night exactly what kind of man you are. I was stupid to expect a shred of compassion from you...'

'Compassion?' He looked at her as though she were mad. 'This is business, black and white, commercially sensible business. Nothing else. If I invested half a billion pounds into failing hedge funds just because a woman I'd slept with asked me to, I would have nothing left to invest.'

The sting of his words whipped her to the core of her soul. It wasn't as though she was under any illusion when it came to his sexual experience but a reminder of the number of women he'd slept with sat like a boulder in her throat. She stared at him for several seconds and then nodded jerkily. 'Perhaps it would be better if you forgot I came, Mr Durante.' She used his surname meaningfully, side-stepping him and moving towards the table where her clutch bag sat discarded.

He watched her stride towards the door with a frown on his face and, though he'd been frustrated by her sudden intrusion, and even more so at the reason for it, he didn't relish the prospect of her disappearing once more.

His lawyers had quarantined the funds for this investment earlier that same day—as chance would have it, he'd been planning to call Laurence that afternoon to finalise the details.

Instead, Jemima had arrived with her fluffy blonde hair and the fringe that hung across one eye making him itch to reach over and push it away so he could regard her properly. Jemima with her defiant eyes and trembling mouth, her vanilla fragrance and tantalising curves. The four weeks he'd spent telling himself how bitterly he regretted falling for her many charms had evaporated into thin air.

He was glad to see her. He wanted to see more of her. The realisations were instantaneous, brought to life by her imminent departure.

'Wait.'

Her hand had curved around the door. He stayed exactly where he was, a desire to appear in control innate to him, even as there was a rival instinct to stalk across the room and drag her into his arms.

'What?' She barked the word with disbelief. 'What do you want?'

It was an excellent question and, if he'd been a different man, perhaps he would have obfuscated, sought cover in a lie. But Cesare was not a man to lie. 'You, *uccellina*. Just you.'

Her eyes flew wide and her lips parted, colour invaded her cheeks and beneath the fine cotton of her shirt her breasts puckered so he could see the definition of her nipples against the fabric. His groin tightened, desire rushing over him.

All his adult life, he'd been in charge. Not once had he slept with a woman and had it morph into something else, and this wouldn't, either. This was just sex, desire plain and simple, but one night hadn't been enough. Perhaps it was the way they'd come together, the surprise of her innocence or the abrupt way he'd put an end to what they were doing. He hadn't been able to think of her without regret and now, here she was in his office, a second chance with her tantalising and impossible to ignore.

He held up a hand, forestalling anything she might say in response. 'Hear me out.' He paced towards his desk, a frown on his face as he thought through what he wanted and how to get it. 'You are worried about your cousin. Fine. You wish me to alleviate those worries by investing in his business right now, today?'

She bit down on her lower lip and nodded, angst so obvious in her eyes.

He ignored it. This wasn't about sympathy. It wasn't about compassion—she'd been wrong to expect either of those qualities in him. This was business, pure and simple. She was an acquisition, just like a company he might wish to buy. True, the terms were vastly different, but if mutually agreeable the professionalism of the deal would be the same.

He spoke slowly, placing his palms on the edge of his desk as he eyed her across the room. 'In business it is normal to offer something in exchange. If I were to buy into his hedge fund, which may very well prove to be a complete waste of my money,' he said, knowing full well the fund was likely to double in value in the next six months, 'then I would expect something in exchange.'

She was quiet. His eyes ran over her face and a rush of excitement surrounded him. He'd thought of her frustratingly often—how come it hadn't occurred to him that he could leverage her situation to give them what they both wanted?

'Have you thought of me since that night?' he asked, his body still, his eyes trained on her face so that he could catch any hint of response, the slightest reaction. He didn't have to look too hard. Her hand lifted to her hair, pulling it over one shoulder, and her expression shifted to one of disbelief.

'Why does it matter?' And then, a second later, 'Have you thought of me?'

'Yes.' He held her gaze when she might have looked away. 'You weren't what I expected.'

Her throat shifted as she swallowed. 'So I'm some kind of an enigma?'

An enigma? Yes, that was it. How else could he explain the fact his mind had frequently wandered back to that night without his consent? 'You could say that.'

'So?' Her eyelids fluttered as she lifted her gaze to his and an ache to possess her again— properly this time—soared in his chest. Yes, he wanted her, and not like last time. He wanted to savour every kiss, every movement, every feeling and sensation. He wanted to do this properly, at his leisure.

'I have a proposition for you. A way to help Laurence and give you and me what I think we both want.'

But one more night wouldn't be enough. Instinctively he knew the fever she'd evoked would be harder to quell in his blood than a single night would allow for.

'I will invest in the fund today, this afternoon—no more due diligence, no more delays—if you agree to my terms.'

She crossed her slender arms over her chest, the gesture drawing his eyes to the gentle swell of her cleavage, so every fibre of his being tightened and shook with need. 'What terms?'

The certainty that he was close to success shot through him. He knew what victory sounded like and it was close at hand.

'Two weeks.' His eyes flared as he delivered the terms.

Her lips parted as a small sound rushed out of her and colour peaked in her cheeks, pale pink, so that she was like a very soft rose petal. She knew exactly what he was offering, but he wasn't a man who was prone to uncertainty, so he felt the need to spell out exactly what he was offering and exactly what he wanted.

'In my bed.'

And now, he stepped out from behind his desk, moving towards the door where she stood, his stride long, his manner intent.

She stared at him as he approached and he relished this—the promise of what was to come. For, as sure as night followed day, she would agree to his terms.

'But why?' The words were whispered, hollow-sounding.

He lifted a finger and pressed it to her lips, keeping her silent. 'I am not interested in a relationship—not with you or any woman.' The words were said coldly, but it was better that she understood, unequivocally, how he felt. As a young man Cesare had sworn he would make a success of himself and relationships didn't factor into that. Sex, yes. Anything more serious? Hell, no. And never with a woman like

Jemima, who was as to the manor born as it was possible to get.

'What I'm offering is a very clearly defined arrangement.' He felt her swallow this time, her lips pursing as she tried to relax her mouth. He fought an urge to slide his finger into the warm cavity, to feel her moistness wrap around him… Soon. He needed her to agree to this and then it would begin.

'Explain it to me,' she whispered, faint of breath.

He took the question as a win. He was close to victory. 'For two weeks you will be by my side. Morning, noon and night, in my bed any time I wish it, charming me, making love to me. You will be, in every way, mine.'

She trembled a little and a husky gasp escaped her lips. 'Why?'

He laughed. 'You really have to ask that?' He pressed his body forward and, when his hard ridges connected to her soft curves, he didn't relent, stepping forward again so she was shuffled back into the door. He pressed her to it, seeing the moment her eyes flared wide as she felt his arousal hard against her body.

'I mean, why would I agree to this?'

He bared his teeth in an approximation of a smile. 'Putting aside the fact you have just told me how desperate your cousin is, and implied you would do *anything* to help him?'

Her cheeks fired pink and her eyes cut through him with something approaching disdain. It was useful—an excellent reminder of who and what this woman was. Aristocratic. Entitled. Spoiled. All the things he'd come to loathe, all of the attitudes and bigotries of which he'd been on the receiving end time and again, before he'd made his fortune and become the kind of man with whom everyone—regardless of their title and wealth—felt a need to flatter and ingratiate themselves. Her disdain was nothing new, and it fired him up now, reminding him why he kept himself well away from women like this.

This was just sex. Sex, business, pleasure, but each separated from the other by the lines he was drawing now.

'I am the only man you have ever slept with,' he said with a lift of his brow and a twist of his lips that was sheer arrogant machismo. 'And there is much you have to learn.'

Her eyes narrowed and she regarded him with

an even greater level of disdain and even a glimmer of dislike. 'How do *you* know you're the only man I've ever slept with?' she prompted.

'I was there the other night,' he reminded her, no dint to his confidence. 'Remember?'

Her voice was soft when she spoke, mellow and husky. 'You were my first lover. It doesn't necessarily follow that you remain my only.'

Cesare—who prided himself on being quick on the uptake—took several seconds to comprehend exactly what she meant. But, when he did, he felt an almighty surge of adrenalin and a burst of male egotism that had him acting without thinking.

'You're lying.' The words ripped from him even as his head swooped down and his lips claimed hers. 'You are lying.' He threw the words into her mouth as his hands curled at her hips, lifting her up and bracing her back against the door.

The idea of another man doing this—touching her, kissing her—flicked something inside him and he was waging a war against a primal instinct of possession, an instinct that went beyond sense and logic, an instinct he couldn't fathom, didn't welcome, yet couldn't deny.

He swore into her mouth and kissed her harder, or perhaps it wasn't a kiss so much as a complete subjugation, a need to show her that he could command her desire and please her more than anyone else on earth.

'What does it matter?' she threw at him, breaking free of his kiss before her lips sought his of their own accord.

What did it matter? Hell, he couldn't say, only he knew it *did* matter, and it fired his determination anew—he would wipe any other man from her mind, he would remove them from her body, he would make her his. For the sheer sake of it. For pride.

CHAPTER FIVE

SHE WAS DROWNING and she didn't care. Water filled her lungs, her eyes, her cells, her heart. She was drowning and there was no point trying not to—she would choose this drowning death a thousand times over. His hands on her body were strong and possessive, his lips unrelenting, his arousal persistent against her so she felt her own need explode in a way that was more fierce than any stick of dynamite, any firework, any flame.

She'd lied to him. Pride had driven her to remove that smug, arrogant look from his face. He might have been right—he was the only man she'd ever slept with, and he had filled her dreams for days and nights on end—but he had no right to look at her and expect her to jump when he snapped his fingers.

He deserved to have his arrogance shaken, his confidence taken down a peg. Beautiful, sexy, smug bastard…

His hands pushed at her blouse, and in his haste he tore the buttons, so one popped clear across the room. She barely noticed; she was just so glad the moment his fingers pushed aside the lace of her bra and cupped her naked breast, his touch instantly familiar and desperately perfect. She rolled her hips, her legs wrapped around his waist, her jeans an unbelievable barrier to what she wanted, what she needed.

And he understood, pushing his cock harder against her, so that even through all the fabric that came between them he found the sweet spot of her nerves and moved himself there, inflating her pleasure, pushing her higher and higher into the heavens. His tongue tormented her mouth, his hands controlled her breasts; she was lost to him and this.

She needed him. After four weeks of being made love to by the phantom memories of Cesare Durante, being held, touched and kissed by the real thing was a heavenly balm.

Pleasure rose, a wave upon which she was travelling, her breath torn from her, need insatiable and fierce. She ached for him—nothing else mattered. In that moment, she wasn't thinking of Laurence, the hedge fund or the deal Cesare had proposed, she was simply a being born of sensation and need.

Lights danced behind her eyelids, bright and persistent, flickering until they became one big inferno, making sight impossible. But who needed sight when there were feelings such as this?

'Please.' She rolled her hips again, her release so close, so tantalisingly close.

'No.' He lifted his head, the word whipping her as though he'd sliced her with a blade.

Her breath was still coming in pants, her eyes awash with desire as she stared up at him in utter disbelief. He eased her feet to the floor, his eyes hard in his handsome, symmetrical face. If it weren't for the dark slashes of colour across his cheekbones, she would have said he had been completely unmoved by what had just happened. But she'd *felt* his response; she knew his desire to be as fierce as her own.

Except now he was looking at her with a clinical detachment, a sense of complete unconcern, as if nothing had even happened between them. He was all business, ruthless, concentrated, intense.

'You will become my mistress. For two weeks.' He held his hand up, two fingers raised. 'In exchange,' he added darkly, 'I will show you a kind of pleasure you can only imagine.'

Jemima swallowed, her traitorous body refusing to listen to sense, refusing to care that he was using her desire to blackmail her.

'I'm not for sale.'

His expression showed mocking amusement. 'Everyone is for sale, for the right price.' He skimmed his eyes over her body. 'You want me to save your cousin? Done. You want me to *please* make love to you?' He mimicked her tone and she winced. 'You want me to touch you all night until you can barely think straight? Done. Choose which of these prices is more palatable to you and we will go with that.'

Her fingers tingled with a desire to slap him, but damn it, he was right. She needed this; needed him. Her eyes showed frustration as they locked with his. She couldn't easily choose *why* she would agree. For Laurence? She would do anything for him. Her future was tied closely to his, but more than that, he was like a brother to her. Yet her love for Laurence had no bearing on her decision.

The temptation she felt to agree to Cesare's proposal had one root only—she needed him and she'd do anything, agree to anything, for that pleasure. Even sacrifice her pride? Apparently.

'And at the end of the two weeks?' she whispered, closing her eyes so as not to see his triumphant expression.

'You disappear from my life—sexually illuminated and your cousin financially secure.'

She swallowed, his words pulling her to pieces. 'And it's that easy?'

'Yes.'

'What if it's not?' She blinked her eyes open now, a frown puckering her brow. 'What if two weeks come and go and you don't want me to leave? Or what if I want to stay?'

His expression was as relentless as a vise. 'Not possible. I offer this and no more. It is a deal, an agreement, no less binding than any of the contracts I enter into on a daily basis.'

She nodded, but her heart did something strange in her chest, lurching from side to side. 'I need to think about it.'

His laugh was like the Niagara Falls emptying on her head.

'What? Why is that funny?'

'It is obvious you intend to say yes. Do not lie to me, now.' He lifted a finger to her lips, tracing their outline before pressing the tip into her mouth. She bit down on it with her teeth, not hard, but in a silent warning that had him laughing once more.

'You are unbelievably arrogant,' she muttered.

'Yes.'

God, he was—why the heck hadn't she been able to put him out of her mind? Why had he somehow got under her skin and into her blood like this? 'I don't even like you.'

His look was one of wry amusement. 'Then it's just as well I'm not asking you to like me.' He moved his head closer towards hers, so when he whispered she could hear every syllable of his words. 'Liking one another has nothing to do with what we are. I am asking you to be my mistress, not my girlfriend. It is a simple yes or no question.'

She swallowed. It wasn't simple, it was complex, but only because she wished she felt more strongly opposed to this. She wished she were outraged or violently offended. She was neither.

In point of fact, she was intrigued and excited. Yes, excited. A month ago, Cesare had woken a part of her that she hadn't even realised was dormant. He'd stirred her to life and, no matter what she might think of him personally, she had no doubt he was just the man with whom to explore this sensual side of herself.

Perhaps she could approach this exactly as he suggested: as a business arrangement. Oh, not in the sense that he was bankrolling Laurence. That had to be removed from her mind. This was a decision about whether she wanted to sleep with Cesare, whether she wanted to become his mistress—for a short period of time. It was about what she stood to gain from this—not financially, so much as physically.

Her eyes clashed with his and something locked in place inside her, something vital. She could make her peace with this situation because deep down she knew that it was her choice. He was providing an option, but she was only accepting because she wanted to.

'I have the Feranti e Caro fashion show next week,' she murmured, hearing herself and knowing there was acquiescence in the words.

'Cancel it.'

Angry heat fired in her belly. 'No way. I can't. This is my career and I won't let them down. I don't ever cancel a show once I've agreed to it.'

His lips compressed, his expression impossible to interpret, until finally he nodded. 'Fine. One night.' His eyes flared. 'Otherwise, you are mine.'

She wanted to tell him that people couldn't belong to people, that the idea of ownership was ridiculous and patriarchal, that it offended every level of her feminist heart. But she knew, even as those words flew through her, that a part of her had belonged to him the moment they'd met, and she wasn't sure she'd ever get it back.

Excitement buzzed through her; pleasure and anticipation, as well. It would have been easy to forget why she'd come to him, easy to forget her cousin and what she owed him.

Cesare made that impossible, though. 'I will advise my lawyers to contact Laurence. It will take a few days for the funds to transfer.' His eyes locked to hers, then he spun away, stalking towards his desk. He scrawled something on the back of a business card then crossed to her once more, his manner strictly business.

'Friday—meet me here.'

She dropped her eyes to the card, reading his confident scrawl.

Hotel Sable d'Or, Cannes.

He pressed a finger to her chin, lifting her face towards his, something in his eyes that spoke of promises and needs. 'Don't disappoint me.'

Her lips parted on a sigh—a sigh that was part promise and all hope. 'I won't.'

And then he dropped his head to hers, this kiss slower, more enquiring, as though he were tasting her, teasing her. It still had the same effect: her knees threatened to buckle beneath her and her mind went blank. It was all too brief, though.

'Dream of me.'

She nodded, because she knew she would, just as she had been, and his laugh was soft. 'I will make you forget whoever it was you slept with after me. I will ruin you for any other man, *uccellina.*'

Thud. Thud. Thud. One foot after the other. Faster. Better. His eyes flicked to his watch, checking his pace and then his heart rate, but only for a second. *Don't take your eyes off the goal*. He dipped his head forward, keeping his frame in its most aerodynamic state, and continued to run. Rome passed him in a blur, as it did every night, his body at one with this ancient city, her secrets breathing into his soul, ancient wisdom soothing him in a way he hadn't known he needed until he'd found his way back here.

He liked to run to the outskirts of the city, to the borderline slum in which he'd spent the first five years of his life. To stare at the building—it was still there—with the peeling paint and the boarded-up windows, the wall with faded graffiti as though even vandals preferred not to come into this part of the city. He liked to listen to the sounds, to breathe in the smells and to remember—this was where he had started in life.

And always at the back of his mind, no matter how hard he ran, no matter how much he achieved, no matter what his bank balance was, Cesare carried with him a latent fear, a certainty that if he didn't keep running, keep working, keep amassing his fortune, he would end up right back where he'd begun—broke, alone, sad and so hungry he could feel the walls of his stomach squeezing in on themselves.

He was thirty-five years old: that time in his life was decades ago, yet the memories were trapped inside him in a way that showed they'd never fade. Despite all that he'd earned, Cesare could never forget the little boy he'd been then—oftentimes grubby, weary, a boy people would cross the street to avoid. How ironic that he could now command the attention of world leaders, of kings and queens and, most importantly, of women like Jemima Woodcroft...

She'd been to Cannes many times and to this hotel, though never to the penthouse. This expansive, stunning living area—stretching the entire footprint of the hotel—was beyond her wild imaginings. Decadent in the French rococo style, with ornate pieces of antique furniture, it was sumptuous and romantic.

The word breathed its way through her mind and she quickly muted it. There was nothing romantic about this. He'd thrown her out of his home, more or less, when he'd realised she'd been a virgin, and a month later he'd propo-

sitioned her right back into his bed. Romantic? Ha!

She strode through the double-height living
room, with its floor-to-ceiling glass windows
framing a view of the moonlit French Riviera in
one direction, with boats lit golden and bobbing
on the gentle waves, and in the other of this
beautiful, billionaire's playground—equally
glamorous hotels, and shops that made this part
of the world so renowned.

For Jemima, though, the pleasure in Cannes
had always been in the gardens.

The city was—and had been for a long
time—home to some of the world's wealthiest
residents, and the public gardens were a testa-
ment to that. Jemima could lose hours alone
in the Jardin des Oliviers, wandering the olive
grove, finding her way onto the perfectly lush
grass and sitting people-watching, a large hat
and sunglasses the perfect disguise to avoid
being easily spotted here, where people were
well-trained in picking out the celebrities in
their midst.

It was a warm, sultry evening and the wind
that lifted off the Bay of Cannes was fragranced with salt. She breathed it in deeply,

trying to calm the furious beating of butterfly wings against her belly.

The money had cleared the day before. Laurence had been like a new man—the stress he'd carried for over a year dissipating completely. *It's going to be okay, Jem. It's really going to be okay.*

And maybe he was right. If the hedge fund returned to the black, then it would mean relief was at hand for Almer Hall, and the enormous debts that encumbered the property. Perhaps, after a decade of fretting about the state of the grand old home and the burden of keeping it in the family, things were finally going to get easier.

The sound of a door clicking had Jemima spinning where she stood in time to see Cesare enter. For the first time since they'd met, he wasn't wearing a suit. Instead, he was casually dressed in dark denims and a pale-blue polo shirt, the collar lifted a little in a way she suspected was a result of movement rather than a contrived attempt at fashion.

His eyes swept the room and landed on her almost as though he hadn't expected her to be there. The second he saw her, he began to move, his body striding towards her as if on autopilot. She stood where she was and all she could think was that she must look like a deer in the headlights. She spent her life projecting an image—she was paid well to do exactly that—but there was something about this man that made it hard for her to act as she meant.

'Hello.' The word emerged soft and husky.

He stopped short, as if waking from a dream. 'Jemima.' A muscle jerked in his jaw as he regarded her with eyes that showed an unmistakable hunger. He swept his gaze over her face, and she was glad she'd dressed up, glad she'd worn her usual armour. A face with the minimum of make-up and a body in a killer dress. Brightly coloured with spaghetti straps, long and floaty, it was somehow sexy without being obvious, and she loved it. His eyes roamed her body in a way it didn't occur to her to mind because her gaze was indulging its own feast, devouring him limb by limb until, satiated, she drew her attention back to his face.

'Here I am,' she murmured. 'One mistress, reporting as ordered.'

'Bought and paid for?'

'Not quite.' She heard the cultured tones

creep into her voice and saw his eyes flash with something like contempt.

'Did you speak to your cousin?'

She nodded slowly. 'He's very pleased.'

Satisfaction crossed Cesare's face. 'I can imagine.' He lifted a hand then, his eyes boring into hers in a way she found impossible to look away from. 'Five hundred million pounds, and likely the need for more in six months.'

It was so much money. The idea that he'd paid that simply to get her back into bed was a strange realisation to grapple with. On the one hand, it was completely flattering—she had no doubt he could have, and had had, any woman he wanted. But it was also troubling, because it was a fortune to gamble if Laurence didn't know what he was doing.

'I'm sure it will return well for you.' Her voice didn't ring with conviction.

'We'll see.' His hands dropped to her shoulders, to the straps there, pushing at them slowly, his expression droll, his eyes holding a silent challenge. 'You're over-dressed.'

Her heart skidded through her chest; her eyes slowly lifted to his as desire slammed into her. 'Am I?'

'I'd prefer you to spend the next two weeks naked,' he said, a hint of amusement in the words.

The very idea of being naked in this hotel, waiting for him, existing for their coming together, filled her with an all-over rush of heat that engulfed her soul in flames.

'And you'd be naked too, I presume?' she responded acerbically, and was rewarded with a smile. A true smile that shifted his whole expression and made her heart thump harder.

'Certamente.'

She hadn't worn a bra under the dress, so when he pushed the straps farther and it slipped to the ground she stood before him in a lace thong and stiletto heels, her hair tumbling about her shoulders.

Cesare took a couple of steps back, his eyes traversing her body with impunity, lingering on the curve of her breasts, the swell of her hips. Everywhere he looked her skin seemed to tingle, as though it was his fingertips dragging across her slowly, feeling her, touching her.

When he lifted his attention to her face, there was accusation in his expression, a look of resentment that made no sense. But it was gone again so quickly that she wondered if she'd imagined it. His cheekbones were slashed with dark colour, just as they'd been in his office when he'd reined in their explosive passion.

She didn't want him to rein in anything now.

'You're wearing clothes,' she pointed out huskily.

His nod was slow. 'Perhaps you should do something about that.'

Her throat felt thick and dry. She stepped out of the fabric of her dress that was pooled at her feet, then kicked off her heels, conscious that she lost a vital few inches in the process, padding barefoot across the room to where he stood not far from her.

Up close, memories slammed into her, the kind of memories that were carried by scent and hormone, so that with every breath he tantalised her and reminded her of what they'd shared.

It was ridiculous to feel shy, but she did— or rather, unfamiliar, because she'd never undressed a man before. Though she'd been surrounded by enough naked men to barely even notice when a bare chest or bottom wandered past, given her line of work, it felt strangely intimate to curl her fingers into the fabric of his shirt and lift it from his body.

Her fingertips trailed across his sides, muscles bunching beneath her touch, until she reached his underarms and had to stand up onto the tips of her toes to lift the shirt the rest of the way. It brought her body close to his, her breasts against his hair-roughened chest, her nipples tightening in immediate response. They were so sensitive, aching for his touch, for his mouth; all over, she ached for him.

She dropped the shirt to the ground, her breath hoarse as she turned her attention to his trousers. Her fingers fumbled on the button and she bit back a curse, moving more slowly, forcing herself to concentrate.

But her fingers weren't cooperating. With a groan of frustration, she dropped to the zip instead, pushing it lower and then attacking the button. It worked. *Hallelujah.* His jeans opened, but it was all too much. She felt as if her nerves were vibrating out of her body. She walked behind him instead, pushing his trousers down from behind, glad for the reprieve from his ever-watchfulness, glad for a moment to regroup.

She crouched down, pushing his jeans to the floor, and he stepped out of them at the same time he turned around to face her. Her clever plan to rediscover her sanity was a complete failure, because she found herself at eye height with his unmistakable arousal. Her eyes lifted to his, uncertainty in them, and he held his hands out towards her. She hesitated for the briefest moment and then put hers in his so he could pull her up, guiding her body towards his.

Their faces were so close, their lips separated by only an inch or two. He stared down at her and her stomach squeezed with anticipation; she felt a rush of adrenalin and a spike of desire. She needed to kiss him. Her body lifted up, her mouth now just a hair's width from his, hunger consuming her.

'I'm not naked yet.' He growled the words, so it felt as though he'd breathed them against her.

'No,' she agreed. 'You're not.' Her hands slid into the waistband of his boxer shorts, pushing at the cotton, curving over his buttocks as she guided them from his body. He stepped out of the fabric and brought his body hard against hers in one manoeuvre. She gasped at the feel of his hardness against her belly.

'And now, your turn,' he murmured, crouching down as he removed her thong. She put a hand on his shoulder as she moved her feet from the elastic.

'Do you know what I've been thinking about since that afternoon in my office?'

'No,' she squeaked as his hands gripped her thighs, moving them a little wider.

'You. And all the ways I plan on making you explode.' His smile was devilish, arrogant, cocky, but it didn't reach his eyes.

'I have been thinking about you here...' He pressed a finger to her sex, and she shivered, her body convulsing at the lightest touch. 'About touching you here...' He flicked his fingers over the most sensitive cluster of nerves at her opening and she gasped. 'And here.' He pushed a finger inside her wet core and she moaned loudly, the hand she'd curved around his shoulder digging in, her nails scoring his naked flesh without meaning to.

'I have been thinking about tasting you here,' he murmured, his eyes lifting to hers, giving her a chance to object, to say something—anything. But she didn't. She simply stared down at his dark head as he pushed forward and ran his tongue along her seam.

Her body reacted fiercely to the unfamiliar possession, so his hands lifted to her hips to steady her, which helped a little. At first. But, as his exploration grew more intense and pleasure began to overtake her entire body, she couldn't stop trembling. Wave after wave of pleasure was making her shake. She dug both hands into his shoulders and surrendered to it completely.

Pleasure built and then she was tumbling off the edges of the earth, falling deep into its core where the heat finally matched that within her body. Her eyes sprang open and she stared out at the ocean, the bobbing boats, the ancient moon, the dark sea, and she felt the strangest sense of relief, of pleasure. And, inexplicably, of rightness.

CHAPTER SIX

HE WAS GONE when she woke up—and no wonder. Jemima pushed back the covers, sitting bolt upright in the luxurious king-size bed, jolting her head towards the window. It was bright outside; warm, too.

'What the heck?' She turned back to her bedside table and reached for her phone, squinting a little as she read the time. It was almost ten! She hadn't slept this late since—probably for ever.

Heat suffused her cheeks—was it any wonder she'd gone into a form of narcoleptic stasis? The things they'd done…all night. She moaned softly, memories slicing through her, warming her, and when she pushed to standing her body felt different. Sore, but in the most delicious way.

She luxuriated in a shower then pulled on a bikini and a flowing kaftan that had been a gift from a designer friend. When she moved into the kitchen in search of coffee, she saw a card propped against the machine, almost as if he'd known it would be the first thing she headed for in the morning.

Gone to work.
I'll be back tonight.
Rest up—you'll need it.

More heat in her cheeks. She read the card again and again, imbuing his husky accent over the words, and desire flared in her belly. She found a smile had stretched over her lips as she poured her coffee, and it didn't drop throughout the rest of the morning.

It was a stunning summer's day. Warm without being unbearable. By mid-afternoon, she was growing impatient to see Cesare. It was ridiculous—they'd made love all night. How could she want him again already?

She grabbed a towel and headed to the pool, determined to work off some of this energy with a swim.

It didn't help. By late afternoon, she knew she needed to pull out the big guns. She changed into workout gear and hit the hotel gym, running ten kilometres before coming upstairs to shower.

She was cooling her heels in the most frustrating of ways.

As the sun began to dip in the sky, she made a cup of tea and settled herself on the sofa, intending to read a few chapters of her book. Without realising it, her eyes became heavy and then she was asleep, completely exhausted, so the sleep overtook her entire body, making her limbs heavy and her breathing soft.

She slept until a hand on her shoulder roused her.

'Oh.' She felt groggy. 'What time is it?'

'Seven.'

'I fell asleep.'

His smile was reflexive. 'Apparently.' He ran a hand over her hair almost as though he couldn't help himself and then dropped it to his side. 'You were tired.'

'Understatement.'

'And now? Are you hungry?'

She blinked, pushing away the last few threads of sleep, and nodded once more. 'Starving. I don't think I've eaten today.'

Something like derision briefly flared in his

features, then he was reaching for her hands, pulling her up to standing. 'Then let's remedy that.'

He took a step back, loosening the top button on his shirt to reveal the thick column of his throat. It was stupid—just a part of his body, a part of the body that everyone had, and yet the sight of his tanned expanse of flesh, the hint of hair she could see at the vee of his shirt, made her mouth go dry.

'Shall we go out? Or eat in?'

'Eat in,' she said quickly without a moment's thought, and then, embarrassed, hastened to add, 'I can't be bothered doing all the stuff.' She gestured towards her face.

'Stuff?' He was already moving across the hotel to the phone in the kitchen.

'You know—make-up, hair.' She scrunched her nose up and his gaze lingered on her face a few seconds too long before he spoke into the phone in fluent French. Jemima had a passable knowledge of the language, but she couldn't keep up with his rapid-fire dialogue.

He covered the receiver. 'Anything you don't eat?'

She shook her head.

He delivered a few more commands then placed the phone in the cradle.

'So why bother?'

She blinked, not understanding.

'With all the "stuff".' He mimicked her gesture, waving his hand over his face.

'Oh.' She moved towards the kitchen on autopilot—more specifically, towards him. A smile hinted at her lips, except it wasn't really funny. 'Have you ever read those blogs or magazines? You know the ones: "stars without make-up"?'

He lifted a brow. 'What do you think?'

It was so ludicrous to imagine him scouring gossip websites or flicking through a glossy that she laughed.

'Is there really such a thing?' he prompted a moment later, reaching into the fridge and pulling out a bottle of wine. He poured two glasses then slid one across to her.

'Oh, yeah, it's a *huge* thing. I guess it's reassuring to know that even celebrities can look like crap without all the effort.'

His scepticism was apparent.

'Hey.' She lifted the wine glass to her lips. 'Don't look at me like that. I didn't start the idea. I've just been the focus of more than my fair share of articles.'

'You?' More scepticism.

'Oh, yeah. Come on, you've read all the stuff. How else do you explain my three phantom pregnancies?' She gestured towards her flat stomach. 'Bad angles, awful lighting, coming straight from Bikram yoga—whatever. Photographers make more selling unflattering images than they do for the ones where I look like I've just stepped off a shoot.'

'But you're beautiful.'

Ridiculously, given that she was a highly paid model and didn't go in for false modesty, her heart gave a little wobble at his praise.

'Objectively speaking,' he clarified, his tone no-nonsense. 'You are a very beautiful woman. You could go down to the Croisette right now and be the most attractive woman there.'

'Okay, stop!' She laughed at the luxuriant praise. 'I know you're making *that* up. I've got chlorine in my hair and I've been for a run so I'm all sweaty.'

His eyes narrowed speculatively and heat buzzed through her veins, so she was only aware of the sound of her pulse in the silence that surrounded them. The longer he looked, the more she felt, and after a few seconds the smile dropped from her lips.

'This isn't vanity,' she said with a small shrug. 'It's professional.'

'Oh?' He sipped his wine, his eyes holding hers over the rim of his glass.

'I represent some of the most prestigious luxury brands in the world. There are all kinds of clauses in my contracts but, even if there weren't, I take my job seriously. I feel an obligation to those companies—I've signed on to sell their brands and I do that best when I'm "Jemima Woodcroft"—not some beach-loving scruff.' Besides, she couldn't exactly afford to lose any of her endorsement deals. True, Laurence's hedge fund might finally be out of trouble, and soon he'd be able to start helping with the exorbitant costs of Almer Hall, but until then she needed every penny she could scrape together.

He was quiet. Self-conscious at his lack of response, she pulled her hair over one shoulder and aimed for a joke. 'I bet you never have to think about this kind of thing when you go out in public?'

'Generally not,' he drawled. Then, thoughtfully, 'So why do it?'

'Model? That's easy. It's what I'm good at.'

'The only thing you're good at?' he prompted with obvious disbelief.

'Maybe.' She moved away from him towards the windows, changing the subject out of habit, and because she didn't like to think about the life she could have led if things had been different. Boats sparkled like fireflies on the sea. 'It's a beautiful night.'

'Yes.' His voice was dismissive, intolerant for her attempt to find lighter conversational ground. 'What else might you have done?'

Her smile lacked amusement. In the reflection of the window, she watched as he crossed the room, coming to stand right behind her.

'I couldn't say.'

'You must have wanted to do or be something other than perennially attractive?'

The words were perfectly banal, but she felt a sting to them.

'Or perhaps not,' he added as an apparent afterthought. 'I suppose you might have wanted simply to be Lady Jemima and marry some lord or duke?'

She couldn't say why, but his question was hurtful. She felt a sting in her chest at that casually worded supposition.

'No.' Her response was carefully flattened of any emotion, though. Bland and unconcerned. 'I wasn't really into that scene.'

'Your parents didn't wish you to marry some titled rich guy?'

Jemima's eyes swept shut for a second, her face pale, and she was glad he was behind her, glad he couldn't see the brief, betraying hint of pain—pain at what her family had once been and what they were now. Pain at the fact her parents had lost their ability at and interest in parenting Jemima when Cam had died. 'They don't really involve themselves in my life.'

'You weren't saving yourself for him, some lord or whatever?'

Jemima spun around to face Cesare and wished she hadn't when the intensity of his expression almost felled her to her knees. 'Absolutely not.' She swallowed and focussed her gaze beyond his shoulder. 'Do you mind if we change the subject?'

'You don't like to talk about this?'

'Not particularly.'

'Your parents or your work?'

'Neither. Both.' A divot formed between her brows. 'Besides, this isn't a psychology session. You propositioned me for one reason and one reason only, remember?' She deliberately brought what they were back to sex, back to the futility in them knowing more about each other. It felt good to control that, good to keep a part of herself separate from him. He wasn't offering beyond this fortnight; why should she bare her soul to him?

'Right.' He nodded slowly, lifting a palm and rubbing it over his stubbled jaw. 'Closed subjects. I get it.' He pressed a finger under her chin, lifting her to face him. 'Did you have a good day?'

Her lips parted. 'Yeah.' A husky admission. 'You?'

He lifted his broad shoulders. 'I bought an airline.'

She blinked at him, sure she'd misheard. 'What?'

'Not a big one. Seventy-one planes. But it's my first move into the air travel industry.'

'So, yesterday you bought half a billion dollars' worth of a hedge fund and today an airline?'

His smile stole her breath. 'Apparently I've been on a spending spree.'

'Apparently,' she agreed, his proximity supercharging her blood.

She moved back to the kitchen, taking a sip of her wine. It was sweet and quite delicious, but she reached for a tumbler and filled it with water, knowing that she couldn't drink wine on its own without losing her head. 'And did the airline come with a convenient mistress, as well?' she couldn't resist asking. 'Someone to move on to after I leave?'

He turned to face her without speaking and they stared at one another for several beats, the silence somehow raw and tense. Jemima's pulse began to rush through her, and she was aware of every movement of his, every shift, every lift. 'Have you done this before?'

He slowly began to walk towards her, and her breath burned in her lungs, her body tense.

'Done what, *uccellina*?'

'Manoeuvred a woman into your bed.'

'Is that what I did?'

She swallowed and nodded, seeing no point

in telling him the truth—that she was exactly where she wanted to be.

'*Blackmailed* would be another word for it,' she drawled, fascinated by the play of emotions in the depths of his eyes. There was no shame, only a hint of triumph.

'No.'

'No?' She frowned. 'You don't agree it's blackmail to tell someone you'll only help the person they love most in the world if they agree to be your mistress for a fortnight?'

Unapologetically, he reached for her, pulling her body to his, and his eyes held something another person might have taken as a warning.

'No, I haven't done this before,' he clarified. 'I do not generally find it necessary to leverage women into sleeping with me.'

A range of emotions burst through her. Surprise, relief, pleasure. 'I suppose you bat them away with a stick.'

His smile was wolf-like. 'I am not lacking for companionship.'

Jealousy was unwelcome and totally unexpected. It cut her chest right open. She stared at him, wondering where the emotion had come from, and why she should even care. She knew what he was like; she'd known even before they'd met that he was someone who went through women like most men went through underwear. She'd known when he'd kissed her that very first time that he was used to crooking his finger and receiving whatever—whoever—the heck he wanted.

'So why'd you blackmail me, then?'

'Why do you think?'

Distractedly, she toyed with the ends of her hair. 'I don't know.'

His hands found the fabric of her shirt and he lifted it. Not slowly this time. It was unceremonious, impatient. 'It's simple.'

She waited silently, watching him, revelling in the feel of the air against her breasts, in his closeness, the heat of possession he could ignite simply by being close to her.

His finger traced a nipple, running around the edges of her flesh, following the line of her dusky areola with lazy intent. His eyes didn't drop, though, and she felt as though he was seeing all the way into her soul.

'You surprised me, and I'm never surprised.'

He moved his body so that she was trapped between him and the bench, so his hardness was against her, and she surrendered to him completely.

'You were a virgin,' he continued simply, moving his attention to her other breast, teasing it with the same feather-light inquisition, the same insufficiency of feel. She wanted him to cup her breasts, to take their weight in his hands; she wanted him to overtake every single one of her senses.

'And you didn't realise.'

'It didn't even enter my head.' His hands curved in the waistband of her yoga pants so he could cup her bottom and hold her against him. She gasped, his arousal so firm at her belly, his touch so commanding, so strong, that she made a primal sort of noise deep in her throat, her needs overpowering her.

'There are dozens of stories about you—your lovers, your lifestyle—but aside from that, you are not a child. No, you are very sensual woman...your body catches fire when I touch you.'

She shivered as he did just that, moving his hand to her womanhood and brushing his fingers over the sensitive flesh there. She tilted her head back and then his lips found one of her breasts, his tongue flicking her nipple until she was moaning, incoherent with the pleasures he promised.

'How is it possible you hadn't done this?' He moved to her other breast, but this time he rolled her nipple in his mouth before sucking it—harder, more forcefully, exactly how she needed it, the pressure setting off an intense cascade of feelings that had her pushing out of her yoga pants without realising what she was doing, needing him in a way that defied reason or sense.

Her hands moved to his waist, pushing at his belt, and he made a husky noise as he lifted his mouth to claim hers, his own hands working furiously to free himself from the confines of his fabric. He layered protection over his cock, and at the same moment Jemima lifted up onto the kitchen bench, he pulled her onto his length, entering her in one firm thrust so she cried out with the relief of his body's return, her muscles squeezing him tight in welcome, her flesh lifting with tiny goose bumps as he moved deeply, perfectly, completely at one with her and her needs.

Her hands tore through his hair, and she

arched her back on an instinctive wave of pleasure, her soul tormented by this in a way she knew she could become addicted to.

His body was so broad, so strong, so completely dominating, and his hands ran over every inch of her, touching her—feeling, worshipping with his touch, until she was like dynamite, lit and ready to explode.

And then, at the moment when she felt as if she would burst, he cupped her bottom and brought her closer to him so he was buried inside her and his kiss was like a command, their bodies melded together. When she tipped over the edge of pleasure into a world that was all sensation, they were so close that she could feel his breath within her soul, she could feel his heart beating against her ribs, and then she felt his own explosion of pleasure, his body racked with the same madness that had commanded hers, his breathing as ragged and urgent, his cries deep and guttural but no less spontaneous.

There was only the sound of their tortured breathing as sanity began to return. Jemima blinked slowly, as though she were waking from a dream when she hadn't expected to be asleep, looking up at him and seeing him through new eyes.

Through eyes that were fogged by desire and satisfaction. By the newness of this. 'Is it always like this?' she asked quietly, hearing the words and wincing at their naivety.

He lifted his head so he could better see her eyes. There was a query in his expression.

'Sex,' she muttered, swallowing her self-consciousness.

His lips lifted in something close to a smile. She studied the lines of his face, the squareness of his jaw, the strength of his nose, the cleft in his chin. It was a face that looked as though it had been sculpted by Michelangelo. It was a face of perfection.

'Like what?' he prompted, his fingers lifting to one of her nipples, twisting it lightly, indolently, with arrogant possession.

Embarrassment grew stronger. 'So...' The word trailed off into nothing. Mortification made it difficult to frame her enquiry. She wanted to know if it was normal to feel as if she needed to rip his clothes from his body whenever she saw him, to fill her with dreams that were positively X-rated, to make her body ache for him in the day when he wasn't near her, and heat with desire at the slightest touch. But what if he didn't feel anything like that for her? What if she alone was mired in an onslaught of unexpected sensual enslavement?

'Sex is thrilling and addictive,' he said, his cock jerking inside her in a way that made her breath snag, because he was growing hard again and her body was tingling with renewed needs. 'But I find this generally fades.' He flicked her nipple with his fingers. 'I have never met a woman I couldn't get out of my system in a night or three.' His eyes probed hers—no, they lanced hers—a look of defiance and determination in his expression. 'This will fade, *uccellina*, and we will both go back to our normal lives soon enough.'

CHAPTER SEVEN

IF ONLY.

Cesare scowled as he scanned the contracts, aware that he was fighting a tic that had him looking at his wristwatch every few minutes.

In the five days since Jemima had arrived at the hotel in Cannes, Cesare had forced himself to stick to his routines. Hell, he hadn't anticipated that would be difficult. He'd flown his helicopter to Rome, arrived at his desk at the usual time, stuck to his meetings and his schedule, because why the hell wouldn't he? He hadn't missed a single day of work since he'd founded Durante Incorporated. It didn't matter that he owned the company and was now one of the richest men in the world. It didn't matter that he employed an army of executives who were undoubtedly more than capable of keeping things going—if not for ever, at least for a few days.

A few days?

The idea spread like wildfire in his veins. A few days with Jemima. No constraints. No having to get up in the morning and leave her sleeping, her beautiful body naked in his bed, her soft murmur of complaint as she felt him roll away from her, as though protesting the necessity of his departure.

As though she wanted him to stay.

What would it be like if he took the rest of the week off? If he woke her up by kissing her breasts, slowly dragging his mouth down her body, his tongue tracing lines across her flesh, tasting her, teasing her, delighting in her responsiveness.

A curse exploded from him as he scraped his chair back and stalked to the window. He stared down at Rome, his chest moving rapidly with the rise and fall of his breathing, something uncomfortable shifting through him as he accepted that this was different from what he'd anticipated, that it was at risk of getting out of hand.

Oh, it was just sex. He knew that. There were myriad reasons it could never—would never—in a billion years be anything else. Not least of all was her aristocratic birth, her air of being to the manor born, which was something he could never tolerate long term. Not having seen what people like her were capable of, or the way they viewed the world.

But more than that, Jemima was dangerous. She was like a drug—something else Cesare had never indulged in. He had legendary self-control; he refused to be tempted by anything that might prove detrimental to his life, his career, his business, his one-eyed focus.

And yet somehow, he'd willingly become hooked on Jemima Woodcroft. It was all the more reason for him to be firm in his routine, to stick to his schedule, not to let her influence him or affect his life in any way. No woman had ever shaken his convictions, no woman had ever so much as tempted him to blow off work and stay in bed for days at a time, as he wanted to with her.

Jemima was a first.

And why?

Va bene, she was beautiful, but that wasn't exactly a novelty—there were many beautiful women in the world, and in any event he wasn't the kind of man to value looks above chemistry and spark. No, it wasn't a looks thing. So what else could it be? Surely her innocence played a part? She'd been a virgin when they'd met and there was a novelty in that, a curiosity, because it made as little sense to him now as it had that night.

A dark emotion burst through him and he pushed away the dark intrusion on his thoughts—the idea of her having bounced from his bed into someone else's, the knowledge that some other man had made love to her after him.

Curiosity was natural. It was hardly a crime for her to have decided to experiment with her awakened sensuality.

And yet Cesare felt a sharp burst of rage that didn't bear examining. It didn't matter. She was his now, and at the end of the agreed upon two weeks he'd let her go and never think of her again.

It seemed impossible to contemplate, in that moment, when Jemima had been all he could think about all day for many days, but he didn't doubt even for a second that he'd succeed.

Because he was Cesare Durante and he hadn't met anyone or anything in his life that he hadn't had the mental fortitude to conquer. Jemima, ultimately, would prove to be no different.

* * *

The bobbing of yachts on the water was a mes-
merising sight—hypnotic, almost—and Jemima
found, as the days wore on, that it hadn't become less so. She sat at the table now, her hands
clasped in her lap, staring at the boats as they
moved gently with the water's pull, not fighting it, surrendering to the tidal ebbs and flows,
the enthusiasm of the water to meet the shore
and recede once more to its oceanic depths,
and she felt a strange affinity to the water. The
currents of this body were stirred by a power
beyond their comprehension but simply obeyed
an ancient, cosmic call.

Jemima was not an ocean, but her pull towards Cesare was no less marked than if he'd
been the moon, drawing her towards him each
night. Five nights in Cannes and she had begun
to understand a few vital and key aspects of
this man's personality.

He was punctual to a fault. She could set her
watch by his arrival back at the hotel and by
the time he left each morning. Every day it was
exactly the same, almost to the minute. From
this it was easy to infer that he liked order and

control, that he was driven to tame every aspect of his environment.

And, just as Jemima's career had led to her making an art form out of being charming without divulging anything she truly thought or felt, she began to suspect Cesare operated on a similar principle. Oh, he was significantly less charming. He was definitely not a man who cared what people thought and therefore he didn't waste time trying to curry good favour. But there was something firm within him, some kind of wall or blockage, something that stopped her from ever feeling that she truly understood him.

That was a *good* thing. Understanding him, knowing him too well, felt like it would be a slippery slope to danger.

And yet, despite that, she'd arranged all this—a table set on the balcony overlooking the bay, candles dotted around the floor and hanging from the ceiling and a three-course meal already in the kitchen so they wouldn't be disturbed.

Not only that, a lick of nervousness was making her fingers quiver a little, so she poured herself a half glass of the fine champagne she'd added to the order, wondering if it might ease her energetic nerves.

Her eyes flicked to her phone, and at the precise moment she expected him the door pushed inwards and she smiled to herself, glad his punctuality hadn't failed him. Her nerves were already stretched to breaking point. She stood, focussing on controlling her outward response, pretending she was at a shoot, assuming a look of cool calm that she definitely didn't feel.

She saw his eyes as they ran over her body—she'd deliberately chosen this dress, the same one she'd worn to the restaurant the first night they'd met, the dress he'd pulled from her body the first time they'd made love. She felt the hunger in his eyes, the need in his body, and her own body trilled in response.

She was actually looking forward to this. Looking forward to sharing a meal with him—not grabbed from the kitchen when hunger finally drove them out of bed but a proper meal, across a table, with conversation and…

And what?

She understood the need for caution. In the back of her mind, she remembered every sentence he'd uttered that told her how temporary this was, how determined he was to resume his normal life as soon as their allotted two weeks were up.

And yet, they were sleeping together. It might not mean anything, in the sense of romance and a future, but it still felt strange to know his body intimately when she knew so little of his mind, his stories, his history and life.

'What's this?' He removed his tie as he crossed the room, hanging it over the back of the chair before stepping on to the terrace. The sun was low in the sky, casting the world in shades of violet and gold, and they bounced off his face so that she had to bite back a gasp at the sheer magnificence of him.

'A table,' she quipped, her voice a little raspy, waving a hand towards it. 'Somewhere you sit when you eat a meal.'

'You don't like it when I feed you in bed?' There was a growl to his words as he pulled her body. Heat burst inside her veins.

'Oh, I like that very much,' she responded with a smile. 'But I thought we'd try something different tonight.'

He said nothing, but his eyes showed a hint

of something—warning, or a wariness, that she instinctively understood.

'This isn't a *date*—relax. I'm not trying to entice you into anything more than the deal we've made.' She sobered, scanning his eyes thoughtfully. 'What's wrong? Is sharing dinner against the mistress rules or something?'

A muscle jerked in his jaw. 'There's a first time for everything.' His smile was barely a lift of his lips. He stepped away from her, reaching for a chair and separating it from the table, holding it so she could be seated. But as she eased herself into it with a grace that was borne of natural instinct rather than professional training, his fingers lingered on her shoulders and he dropped his head so he could whisper in her ear, 'Let's see how long we last.'

A *frisson* of anticipation straightened her spine and her breasts tingled, her nipples tightening in ready response to his huskily voiced promise. But it was a challenge, a throwing down of the gauntlet, and she wanted to prove him wrong, to prove to both of them that they were capable of having a conversation that wasn't punctuated by sensual need.

He took the seat opposite, but didn't shift forward, so he was far enough across the table to regard her with a kind of scrutiny that filled her body with little electric shocks.

'I gather you don't generally date the women you sleep with?'

His nostrils flared as he exhaled. 'You have an unusual interest in my previous lovers.'

The accusation smarted. She shook her head in an instant denial. 'Not at all. I'm just trying to understand how this usually works.'

'Why?'

Her smile was rueful and lacking humour. 'So I know what to expect after you?'

It was both the wrong—and the right—thing to say. His features cracked with something dark and intense, something like absolute, visceral rejection. It was the first time in Jemima's life that she realised she could get some kind of dark pleasure from an emotion like envy. It was over in a heartbeat, his expression cleared of anything, but it had been there, she was certain of it. He didn't like the idea of her being with someone else. It was why he'd made such a big deal about the other lover who—out of pride—she'd invented.

'I'm not a good barometer of normal when it comes to relationships.'

'Why not?' In spite of her best intentions, curiosity flared to life.

'Because I don't have relationships,' he drawled, the words mocking, but she refused to be cowed.

'Why not?'

He reached forward and topped up her champagne flute without touching his own glass.

'I don't have time.'

She frowned. 'You have as much time as anyone else.'

'My work is my life.' He lifted his shoulders, dismissing her line of enquiry.

'Why?'

His eyes flared briefly with surprise, but he tamped the reaction down quickly enough. 'I employ over eighty thousand people around the world. You don't think I have a reason to be busy?'

'Mmm…' She tilted her head to one side, considering this. 'But you must have people who report to you, a chain of command.'

His eyes narrowed. '*Certo.* But I oversee it. Every aspect.'

For no reason she could think of, a shiver ran down her spine. There was such a mark of determination in his voice that it almost felt like a warning.

'Every aspect?'

'This surprises you?'

Her smile was instinctive. 'Actually, it doesn't.' She dipped her head forward a little.

'No?'

'That you're a control freak? Oh, I think that's patently obvious.' She lifted her gaze then, fixing him with a curious stare. 'Look at the way you manoeuvred me into your bed.' It was a joke, said with a smile, but his expression sobered for a moment.

'I presumed you were a part of the deal that night. I honestly thought you'd come with the intention of flirting with me, of seducing me.'

'I didn't.'

His lips flickered, a smile returning to his face. 'No?'

'You know that's not what happened.' She reached for her water and took a sip. 'Laurence wanted that night to feel social. Truth be told, I think he was probably intimidated as all heck at the idea of meeting you and thought I might make that a bit easier.' She bit down on her lip. 'It's not like he threw me to the wolves—or wolf, in this case.'

Amusement sparkled in Cesare's eyes. 'And yet, here you are, in the midst of the wolf's den.'

'I don't think wolves live in dens.'

'They rear their young in them.'

Surprise at his knowledge had her arching her eyebrow. 'How do you know that?'

'I have a place in Alaska. I go there when I need to work without disruption. A few times a year at least. I learned very quickly that if I didn't become an expert in the local wildlife I wouldn't live very long.'

'What's it like?' she asked, momentarily distracted.

'Alaska?'

She nodded. 'Your place there.'

'It's… You would hate it,' he laughed ruefully, the sound doing strange things to her nerve endings.

'Why?'

'Because it's as far from this as you can imagine.' He waved a hand around the balcony, so beautiful, so luxurious, at the boats bobbing in the background, the air of wealth that was everywhere you cared to look in Cannes.

'It's an old log cabin, built some time in the sixties. It's in the middle of nowhere—you have to either hike for twelve hours to reach it, or you can fly in and land on the lake. The forest is too thick to bring even a helicopter down. When I bought the place, there was no kitchen, no bathroom, nothing. Eventually, I added a small room with basic amenities—no hot water, though—and there's now a small solar-powered generator that means I can run a light and a fridge.'

'Wow.'

'You cannot imagine me there?'

'I didn't say that.' The first time she'd met him, hadn't she been reminded a little of a wild animal? Though he dressed himself in bespoke Savile Row suits, he was clearly a man ruled by passions, powerful in a way that was wild and untamed. 'What do you do while you're there?'

'I work, *uccellina*.' The words held a gentle reminder. 'And sometimes I fish.'

'How can you work? Is there cell reception?'

'Some kinds of work require a complete lack of interruption. I do my best strategising out there. It's where I tend to have big-picture re-alisations.'

'So you can see the forest for the trees?' she prompted, a smile playing around her lips.

'Exactly.' He rewarded her pun with a grin of his own.

'It sounds kind of amazing.'

He laughed, dismissing her conclusion. 'I think you would truly hate it. There are bugs and bears and leeches and there is not a lot to do.'

She bristled at the implication contained in his words. 'And because I'm a model I can't also like the outdoors?'

'Because you are a model, or because you were raised in a particular way.' He said the words with undisguised scorn that had a thou-sand questions filling her mind. 'Take your pick.'

'What do you know about the way I was raised?'

His expression was darkly speculative. 'I can imagine.'

'I doubt that.'

'Let's see. Your parents were proud of you but somewhat removed from your day-to-day life. You had a nanny, possibly two, who taught you from a young age—languages, reading and etiquette, because old-fashioned manners mattered almost more than anything else to your parents. You were sent away to school at some point, though you never had much pressure put on you to achieve academically because your future was secured irrespective of your grades. You were encouraged to socialise in a certain set, with your parents ensuring you spent your time with "suitable" children. You received an allowance—a generous one—and knew you had a trust fund waiting for you. All of your closest friends were of a similar social standing to you. Am I wrong in any of this, *uccellina*?'

He wasn't. In fact, his rendition of her childhood was so accurate that a shiver danced over her spine. The one thing he'd missed out was the loneliness she'd felt after Cameron had died. Loneliness at having lost a beloved older brother, her companion and friend, and loneliness at the way her parents had seemed to withdraw from her, pulling back so she was an island in the midst of everyone's grief, completely set aside from the world. Only Laurence had understood—Laurence, who had been close in age to Cameron, who'd considered him one of his closest friends.

Her voice shook a little, the effect of his summary cutting deep. 'And, because of this, you think I can't enjoy the outdoors?'

'You tell me,' he invited.

She breathed in air that was fragranced partly by the salt of the ocean and partly by his masculinity, and her body responded, her heart pounding with the intensity of her pulse.

'I travel a lot for work.' She pushed aside the troubling memories of her childhood, but a frown lingered on her face. 'But always to places like this. I'm in Milan so often, I might as well be a local.'

His expression could almost have been described as triumphant. She continued before he could speak.

'But in each of these cities I make it my mission to find the gardens.'

He leaned forward a little, surprise obvious on his features, and she felt a burst of satisfaction at having confounded his expectations in some small way. 'The gardens?' he repeated, as though perhaps something had been lost in translation.

She made a noise of assent. 'The gardens. And, whenever I can, I slip away and lose myself in their little corners and hidden pockets. I walk amongst the flowers and I smell them and touch them.' She smiled, her tone conspiratorial. 'Sometimes, I even pick them.'

His own eyes lifted a little at the corners.

'Just one or two, and I take them back to my hotel and put them in a little glass on the window ledge so I can look at them for as long as I'm in town. So it's not like they're dying in vain,' she added with another smile, her blood heating when his eyes thudded to the twist of her lips.

'This I didn't realise.'

'I feel far more at home in gardens than I do in the city,' she said with a lift of her shoulders. 'I always have done.'

'Yet you live in London?'

She slid her gaze back to his face, to those eyes that saw too much. 'It's a good base for someone who travels a lot.'

He dipped his head in silent concession, but when their eyes met she felt a rush of adrenalin, a surge of need that almost overpowered her.

'I ordered dinner. It's in the kitchen.' She

stood a little abruptly, so she took a moment to calm her flustered nerves. 'I won't be long.'

She'd half-expected him to follow behind, to pursue the line of questioning, given that she hadn't really answered him, but he didn't, and she was glad. Glad for space, glad to have room to breathe, to gather her thoughts.

A tray of seafood had been expertly prepared. Oysters, scampi, scallops, calamari. She lifted the stainless steel lid from the platter and moved back to the balcony, her heart giving a little skip when her eyes landed on Cesare once more. He sat with his legs wide, his frame relaxed in the chair, his eyes fixed on the view over the bay, so she had a few seconds to observe him in that moment of unguarded repose. Except he wasn't unguarded; not really.

There was a tightness and readiness about him that seemed ever-present. As though he never really relaxed. Even his time spent in Alaska was probably spent like this—tightly coiled and ready to pounce.

He turned to her almost immediately so she skidded her eyes away and pasted a smile on her face, placing the platter of seafood in the middle of the table. Before she could take her seat, his hand curved around her wrist, holding her steady. His eyes searched hers thoughtfully, probing, reading, and she held her breath without realising it.

She wondered if he was going to speak, but he didn't. He simply looked, and she felt as though the earth was tipping a little, making it hard to keep her balance.

It was the work of an instant. He dropped her hand, smiled in that way he had that was more a replica of a smile than a genuine look of pleasure, and turned his attention to the food.

'When is your fashion show?'

She blinked, her mind temporarily blank before she recalled the Ferante e Caro runway she was committed to take part in.

'Saturday afternoon.'

He nodded. 'In London?'

'Yeah.'

Silence. She watched as he lifted an oyster from the tray, ate it then placed the shell down. 'So why did you come with Laurence that evening?'

'I told you, he thought it would be—'

He shook his head. 'That's why he asked you. Why did you accept?'

'Because he asked me to,' she said after a slight pause, spearing a piece of calamari with her fork. 'And because he's my cousin.'

His eyes narrowed. 'It's more than that.'

'Oh?'

'You were anxious about the hedge fund.'

She bit down on her lower lip. She was wary—wary of saying too much, of betraying Laurence's trust. And yet she felt herself wanting to open up to Cesare. She trusted him in a way she wasn't sure he deserved. 'Yes.' It was a closed off answer.

She reached for her champagne, sipping it slowly. Then she added, 'He's worked hard. I didn't want to see him lose it all.'

She could practically see the wheels turning. 'But you could have afforded to bail him out.'

'Half a billion pounds' worth?' She refuted that with a grimace. 'Not anything like it.'

'Your parents, then? Your aunt and uncle?'

Briefly, her eyes swept shut, and she saw her parents. She saw them as they were now, so pale and weak, worn out by grief and its relentless toll, weathered by life in a way only those who had walked a path like theirs could understand. And, out of nowhere, she saw them as they'd been then.

Before.

Vibrant and happy, always throwing parties and entertaining, laughing and dancing in the corridors of Almer Hall.

'No.' Her answer, again, was short. 'No one could help him.'

It undoubtedly sparked more questions, but suddenly she was a little worn out herself. This had been a foolish idea.

She was trying to turn a sow's ear into a silk purse, and to what end? This was what it was.

A short relationship—no, not even that. She didn't know the word to describe their agreement, but she inherently understood its limitations and the fact it wasn't a real relationship.

With a heart that was suddenly heavy and a body that was as much Cesare's as ever, she moved around to Cesare's side of the table. 'On second thought, I think we should eat dinner later.'

CHAPTER EIGHT

SHE WAS TRANSFORMED.

Cesare watched as Jemima moved the length of the runway, her body like silk floating in the breeze, so elegant and effortless, her steps more like a ballet, a glide. The appeal of the clothes was dwarfed by her beauty, their design made insignificant by her universal appeal.

Her hair had been braided and looped around her head, and she wore subtle make-up: perfect, immaculate. She was irrefutably stunning, but from where he sat in the front row he ached to reach up and pull her hair loose, to tousle it about her shoulders and smudge her lipstick, as he loved seeing it after their kisses. He wanted to kiss her until her mascara had been blinked loose and her cheeks were pink despite the foundation. He wanted her to be *uccellina* again, not this—Jemima Woodcroft.

She paused at the end of the runway, spinning slowly, her smile different from the other models'—she had the ability to light up a room, and he was certain he wasn't the only man present who felt that her pleasure was all for him.

To confirm this, he looked around, his eyes drifting through the audience. It was predominantly women, but everyone—male or female—was transfixed by Jemima. She was famous around the world but amongst these people—fashion devotees—she was like a goddess and they stared at her accordingly.

His gaze wrenched back to her and now he paid proper attention to the outfit, to the gauzy, transparent nature of the skirt that showed her slender legs and hinted at the pale underwear she had on. The blazer was structured and navy-blue with brass buttons but she wore nothing beneath it, and the hint of her cleavage was displayed by the vee at its neck.

He continued to watch her, an expression on his face that anyone in attendance might have regarded as bland—mildly speculative, at most—even when something was stirring to life inside him, beating hard like a drum against his chest.

She looked beautiful, and she was there for

all the world to see. He wasn't used to a sensation of jealousy, nor the tight grip of possession, but he recognised it, just as surely as he recognised the desire to go onto the stage and wrap her in his arms, throw her over his shoulder and carry her back to Cannes. But this was her life—her real life—and he had no place caring how people looked at her, nor wondering if they were mentally stripping her naked.

His mood didn't improve as the night wore on. He was glad when the fashion show wrapped, glad when a thin man dressed all in black and holding a clipboard came up to him, a deferential expression on his face. 'Mr Durante? Jemima's asked for you to come backstage.'

He stood, moving through the crowd, past security and into a crowded dressing area. The noise was deafening. Models, models and more models, all in a state of undress. His eyes scanned the room, looking for only one. She was changed already, into a pair of skinny leather trousers and a silk camisole that showed the outline of her breasts and the slender fragility of her arms and shoulders. Her hair was loose around her face, just as he'd ached to see it.

'Hi.' There was a shyness to her as she saw

him approaching and paused mid-way through unclipping an earring.

His first instinct was to tell her how well she'd done, that she'd been beautiful, that she'd been captivating, but he said none of those things. Surely she already knew them to be true? And saying them felt wrong, given what they were to one another.

'Did you enjoy the show?' she prompted, removing the earring and placing it on the glass shelf behind her.

Had he? He didn't get a chance to answer. Two women came over and wrapped Jemima in their arms, the floral fragrance of their perfume almost overwhelming. 'You ready, babe?'

Jemima's voice stood out, so cultured and elegant. 'I will be soon. Just give me five, okay?'

One of the other models turned to regard Cesare, her eyes inspecting him with slow curiosity.

'Who's this?'

'Just a friend,' Jemima rushed out, her cheeks heating with pink. He wondered at his impulse to contradict her—they weren't even friends. Could he blame her for not knowing exactly how to define their relationship?

'You should bring him along,' the other one purred.

'I might. Five minutes, okay? Tell Larry I'll be out soon.'

'Hurry. I need a Ginsecco.'

They disappeared as quickly as they'd arrived.

'The after-party,' Jemima explained.

'Ginsecco?'

'Prosecco and gin.' She leaned closer, a smile making her face so familiar that his gut squeezed. 'Half of one is enough to make me loopy.'

'Jem?' A male voice this time. Cesare turned around to see a man powering towards her. Not a model—he was too rugged and unkempt for that. 'Bloody hell, it's been an age. You killed it tonight, babe.'

Cesare took a step back, crossing his arms over his chest, so he wasn't even sure if the other man noticed him when he drew Jemima into his arms and pressed a kiss against her lips.

Her eyes flared wide, though, and flew to Cesare, so he had only a second to tamp down on his first instinct—to rip the other man off

Jemima forcibly. With his fist. Was it possible that this was the guy she'd slept with after him? He certainly seemed comfortable with her; their body language could pass as that of lovers.

'You're coming, right?'

She nodded. 'Yeah. Just for one drink.' She lifted her finger in the air to gesture the solitary number and the other guy hooked his fingers around hers, pulling her hand to his chest. 'One of these days you're going to let your hair down. I hope I'm there to see it.' He grinned, a grin that was pure lascivious flirtation, and then he kissed her again quickly, walking away. 'See you at the bar.'

Jemima had the decency to look embarrassed as she closed the gap between them. She lifted a hand to Cesare's chest, staring at it rather than him. 'Sorry about Tim. He's a photographer.'

He didn't say anything.

'The party's just around the corner, in Knightsbridge. Do you want to come in our limo?'

'No.' The word was out before he could analyse it. 'I have work to do.'

'Oh.' Her expression was crestfallen. 'I have

to go—it's expected of me, contractually—but I generally only stay for one drink. Are you sure you don't want to…?'

'No.'

'Oh.' She looked away, turning towards the door where some other guy was waving to her, gesturing for her to join him. 'Well, I can come to your place after,' she murmured. 'I'll be an hour, hour and a half max.'

Temptation dragged on him, a temptation that made him wary because he wasn't interested in anything other than Jemima's body, and only for a limited time. He needed to control this, to remember that this was about sex—the pleasure and hedonism of no-strings sex. She wasn't his real world any more than he was hers.

'There's no need.' He lifted a hand, touching her hair as he'd wanted to while he'd watched her move down the runway. 'We had a deal, remember? This is your night off.'

He thought he'd feel better. He'd thought reminding her of their agreement, the terms, of the role she was fulfilling in his life, would make him feel in control again, would make him feel powerful. But the confusion on her features that was eclipsed by hurt as his meaning dawned did the exact opposite. He wished he could swallow the words back up.

There was courage in her look as she met his eyes. 'What if I don't want a night off?'

Damn it. Powerlessness surrounded him. He moved his hand so his thumb ran over her lower lip. Her eyes fluttered closed, her lashes forming two perfect fans on her face. 'It's what we agreed.' He took a step back. 'My jet will be waiting for you tomorrow.' He slipped a card into her palm with the details of the hangar and his assistant's number. 'Just call when you're ready to fly out and my driver will collect you.'

She dropped her gaze to the card for a second and then looked back at him.

'That's what you want?'

What he wanted? It was getting harder to answer that, but there was always his office, his livelihood, his determination to succeed. These were things that would never wane.

He dropped his lips to hers, buzzing them for the briefest moment. 'Goodnight, *uccellina*. Dream of me.'

The hurt was gone from her features. Now there was defiance as she shrugged her shoulders, turning her body from his, moving towards her friends while lifting her head over her shoulder to call, 'Maybe. Maybe not.'

She dreamed of him in that strange way of haunted dreams, where the fragments seemed so real that she couldn't say if she was asleep or awake. She dreamed of his hands on her body, his lips against hers, his arousal inside her. She dreamed of him, and she writhed for him, and she woke up with a need she couldn't quell. It was a warm day in London, the kind of day that made her ache to be back at Almer Hall, where she could dive into the ancient pond, surrounded by mossy pavers and arum lilies, then turn onto her back, staring up at the sky until the sun formed little circles against her eyelids.

She'd done it a lot after Cameron had died. She'd wanted to escape the house, her parents, their grief and their arguments. She'd wanted to escape the whole world. In the pond, with its murky darkness, its ancient shape, she'd found a world all her own. In the water, she'd been weightless, her ears dipped below the surface so she couldn't hear anything except the beating of her own heart.

In the pond, she'd found peace when her

whole world had been falling apart. She'd found relief from summer's bite and loss's tight grip— the water had made her whole again.

The sun stretched across her bedroom now, long and blade-like, brighter than a star. She lifted her hand, stretching her fingers in its path, and sighed.

Cesare filled her pores, her mind, her soul, her every thought. He was a fever in her blood.

She pushed the duvet back, showering restlessly and dressing quickly—a pair of denim cut-offs and an oversized shirt that had a habit of falling off one shoulder.

Her need for him was insatiable, but there was no point rushing. He'd be working today, despite the fact it was a Sunday, and the thought of returning to their Cannes love nest with no Cesare in sight wasn't a particularly palatable one. She might as well spend the day catching up with friends, seeing as she was in London anyway, and fly out in the afternoon.

In fact, she made a point of going about her life, business as usual: tidying her flat, lunching with her closest girlfriends. She didn't tell any of them where she'd been, nor who she'd been with. It was easy enough to say she was on location for a shoot—she travelled so much for work no one really thought to question it.

Despite the fact she kept herself busy, the day passed interminably slowly. As her cab cut through London in the afternoon—she'd refused to call his driver, to appear as though she couldn't manage to get herself to the airport— she admitted to herself that she'd spent the day in a sort of a trance. It was as though her life, her world, was being viewed through a piece of glass smeared in butter. Everything was blurry and impenetrable. She'd been going through the motions but nothing had felt vibrant or right.

It was the dream that had unsettled her. That, and his comment the evening before, which she'd tried not to think about.

'We had a deal, remember? This is your night off.'

All day she'd pushed those words away, refusing to focus on them, but now as she approached the airport they found purchase in her brain and she couldn't quieten them.

'This is your night off.'

She knew what they were, what she'd agreed to, yet his calm reminder of that tightened around her throat like a vise, so she could barely breathe. As though they could so easily be reduced to a simple arrangement, a contract, she as someone who got 'nights off'. The idea of willingly choosing to be away from him… A shudder ran the length of her spine, a sense of foreboding, because very soon she'd no longer be a part of his life. To Cesare, this was just business, and she was a fool to have forgotten that, even for a moment.

It hurt, but the pain was good. She held it to her chest because it was like a shield—so long as she remembered the truth of what they were, so long as she kept in mind the only thing he'd ever want from her was her body, then she could take the best of what this was, enjoying the sensual pleasure without letting her emotions—her heart—get even remotely entangled.

His fingertips traced invisible circles over her shoulder, waking her softly. Her eyes felt heavy and she blinked them several times to clear sleep from their depths. Disorientation followed. It was warm, as it had been the day before, and she remembered the pond at Almer Hall as though she'd actually been there, so vivid was her recollection. Except she hadn't been; she'd been in London, and she'd been alone.

Craving Cesare.

And now she was back in Cannes, her body his once more, his body hers. Heat warmed her cheeks as she recalled the night before. He'd been waiting for her when she'd returned to the hotel. She hadn't made it four steps into the room before he was dragging her to his body, stripping her clothes, lifting her against him and making love to her as though both their lives depended on it.

'What time is it?' Her words were groggy, infused with exhaustion from a night of passionate love-making.

No, not love-making—sex, she corrected internally.

'Early. I'm going for a run.'

She frowned. He ran every morning, but he'd never woken her beforehand.

'Do you have to?' She rolled onto her side so she could see him better and caught a look of something like disapproval briefly cover his face.

'I run every day.'

Her smile was teasing, her hand lifting to

his shoulder. She pushed him onto his back in the same motion she straddled him, bringing her naked torso down over his chest so her nipples brushed his firm muscles, his hair, and she felt a thousand little blades of desire shoot through her. 'Why don't you *not* run today?' She moved her sex over his hard arousal and his eyes flashed closed.

A rush of power filled her. She bit down on her lower lip as she reached past him to the nightstand where he kept a stash of condoms. Her fingers caught one and she ripped the foil square open with her teeth, her eyes hooked to his as she wriggled down his body. Eye level with his arousal, she risked another glance at him, only to find him watching her intently. Uncertainty shifted inside her but mostly there was still that rush of feminine power, and instincts that had been genetically programmed were now rushing to the fore.

When she shaped her lips over his tip, she felt his body clench, his breath drawn in one ragged intake. She ran her tongue down his length, feeling the pulsing of him, delighting in his obvious pleasure and the feel of him in her mouth.

Her exploration was slow, curious. She'd never done this before and she wanted to enjoy it. She took him in her mouth and listened to his breathing, his guttural moans. She felt when his hands lifted to her hair, tangling in its length, and when his body jerked she smiled and kept going, knowing that she was driving him wild and delighting in that.

But then his hands were tracing her arms and he took the condom from her fingertips, pushing her away as he rolled it over his length, and before she could respond he was pulling her higher, grabbing her hips and guiding her onto his length, holding her down on top of him so he filled her completely. Now it was Jemima's turn to moan as he took over, shifting his body to thrust into her, deeper, hungrier, his hands on her hips firm, guiding her as he wanted her and as he knew she needed him.

And then his hands released her, leaving the tempo up to her, so she could lift her body on his length and satisfy her cravings as his hands ran over every inch of her, feeling her flesh, tormenting her, curving around behind her, exploring her buttocks before lifting to her breasts, cupping their soft roundness. His fingers tormented her nipples, as he obviously knew she adored, squeezing their sensitive tips until she was whimpering with the overpowering sense of pleasure that was tearing her apart.

It was beyond sublime. She arched her back and tilted her head, her eyes finding the ceiling as pleasure detonated through her, through every nerve ending.

'This is...' She had no words. But she was sure he must know, sure he must feel it, too—that he must feel like the world had stopped spinning just for them.

'Great sex,' he supplied as he tilted his hips and thrust into her harder, his hands dropping to her waist again, holding her on his length as he climaxed with a guttural roar.

Blood rushed through her veins. Her heart was on overdrive, her breath was burning and she was tingling all over. *Great sex.*

He was right. This was great sex. Just as he had often. With other women. Just as he'd go on having with other women when their time together was over.

It was a sobering thought, dragging her back to earth, so she lifted off him and collapsed onto her back, the reality of this unfolding through her mind.

He shifted and she waited for him to leave the room, to go for his run. So, when he brought his body over hers, their eyes level, it was a surprise she hadn't braced for.

'Don't you have a run to do?'

'It will keep,' he said, kissing her then, slowly, exploring her mouth as though the kiss could tell him secrets, as though the kiss could fill him with understanding.

He trailed his lips over her body, in the valley between her breasts, lingering there so she held her breath, aching for him all over.

'You were beautiful the other night.'

She couldn't think. He shifted lower, his mouth on her stomach, his tongue circling her navel.

'On the runway. Transfixing.'

'Oh,' she moaned, her nerve endings jangling.

'But you already know you're beautiful.'

His words were said with a smile but she felt something beneath them, something she didn't understand. His tongue flicked against her sex and she bucked, her whole body responding to the intimacy of his kiss. His hands curved around her thighs, pushing her legs wider, and she moaned.

'Was that the guy you slept with after me?'

The question came completely out of left field, and all the more so for the way his mouth was driving her body to another climax, his tongue exploring her slowly, sensually, so that coherent thought was almost impossible.

'What…guy…?'

The words were gasped between her teeth and he pulled away, moving his tongue to her inner thigh so she flinched as he kissed her sensitive flesh there, and she ached for him to bring his mouth back to her sex, back to the very core of her being.

'After the show, in the grey shirt.'

'Tim?' He was a hands-on, flirty guy in general, but they'd only ever been friends. 'No.' It was a groan. Now his hand moved to her flesh, his finger pushing inside her so that she bucked again, lifting her hips in an instinctive welcome to his proximity.

'No?' His finger swirled and she whimpered low in her throat.

'He's…just a friend.'

'So who was he, then?'

'Who?'

'The other guy.'

She dropped her hands to his hair, running them through it, pleasure like a blade pressing against her. 'Please.' The word fell from her lips.

He relented, running his tongue over her womanhood so that pleasure filled her, release close at hand. But his question hovered on the periphery of her mind and a tumbling sense of shame rolled through her.

She'd lied to him. It had been a moment of silly pride, an embarrassment, a desire not to have him think that he'd been the sum total of her sexual experience. In the heat of the moment, she'd thrown it at him to unsettle him, but now she wished she hadn't. She wished she'd owned her inexperience without apology.

'Was he good, Jemima?'

The question made no sense. His tongue slid over her nerve endings; she groaned.

'Did he make you shout his name?'

She shook her head, needing to deny this, to tell him she'd made it up.

'Don't…he…it wasn't…'

And then he was bringing his body higher,

his eyes latching to hers, his expression like thunder. 'On second thought, perhaps I don't want to hear about him.'

Cesare entered her then, swift and intent, and she cried his name into the room, but he kissed her, swallowing the words, his mouth hypnotising.

Their bodies moved in unison, the possession mutual, the insanity all-encompassing, and they exploded as one, satiation enveloping them both, filling them both and tearing them apart all at once. He rolled off her, his breathing loud, and she pushed up to study him, her own pulse still tearing through her. She was out of breath—her fierce desire had pushed it all from her system—but she needed him to hear her, to understand.

She couldn't say why it mattered, but not being honest with him felt completely counter-intuitive. 'I didn't sleep with anyone else.'

He rolled his head towards hers, his expression giving little away.

She found it hard to meet his eyes but she kept speaking, not backing down from the decision she'd made, from what she knew to be the right thing. 'You were so arrogant and self-assured, and I hated the fact you thought you could click your fingers and I'd come running, so I made it up.' Heat bloomed in her cheeks. 'I didn't think you'd care, anyway. I definitely didn't think you'd ever bring it up again.'

His finger lifted her chin so her eyes were forced to meet his.

'I'm the only man you've ever been with?'

The masculine arrogance of that question was obvious and she rolled her eyes in response. 'Yes.'

His grin was her reward. Sexy, arrogant, devilish. 'You are mine,' he said simply, and her heart did a funny little two-step.

'I'm not anyone's,' she countered, and the words felt strange in her mouth, her tongue reluctant to frame them.

'You are mine,' he said again, and this time she didn't bother denying it. 'For now, at least.'

CHAPTER NINE

HE DIDN'T WANT to be in his office.

He pushed up from the desk, pacing to the window, his mind full of Jemima. Full of her confession earlier that day.

'I didn't sleep with anyone else.'

Hell, he felt like he was floating. She was all his. He was the only man she'd been with. It shouldn't have mattered—he hated that it did—and he knew he had to ignore the rush of pleasure that was pounding through him now. Two weeks had somehow whittled down to five nights. Soon he would let her go, watch her walk away and know it to be the end.

He looked around his office, a sombre expression on his face. He travelled often—it wasn't as though he lived in this one single office—yet here in Rome was his headquarters, and it tethered him.

To take time off, to spend that time with Jemima, was foreign and unpalatable and yet his body craved her—*he* craved her. It wasn't about *wanting* her, though, so much as about giving himself every opportunity to get her out of his system. Frankly, he was surprised that hadn't already happened. Usually, two or three nights with the same woman was more than enough. The first flare of passion was met, answered, satiated and disposed of and then his interest waned.

He'd never wanted a woman like this.

He'd never woken up craving someone to the point of distraction. He'd never struggled to keep his mind on his day, his meetings, his work. He controlled his thoughts with ruthless determination, always, but this time it was harder. With Jemima, it was harder.

Damned near impossible, in fact.

He had to work harder, that was all. He compartmentalised all aspects of his life. Grief from the loss of his mother lived inside him, but tucked away in a small space he rarely accessed. So too did childish hurt from being made to feel as a young boy that he hadn't been good enough. Wanting Jemima was simply another box he would have within him, and the same discipline he brought to all aspects of his life would mean he wasn't beholden to it.

Not after this week was up.

It was a resolution that stayed with him all day until he returned to the penthouse, saw her and felt a rush of longing that refused to be shaped. It infiltrated every cell of his body and overtook him entirely.

She was standing in the middle of the kitchen, except it would be more accurately described as a disaster zone. Smoke filled the space, despite the fact the doors to the balcony were thrown wide open, a bag of something like flour had spilled over the bench top, there was a broken bowl at her feet and, when she lifted her gaze to his face, her cheeks were beautifully flushed, her eyes wide.

'Don't say a thing,' she muttered darkly, words that were somewhat belied by the rueful smile on her lips.

His own mouth lifted in response. 'Doing a little redecorating?'

She poked her tongue out at him and another wave of need assaulted his body.

'For your information, this was a *nice* gesture,' she muttered.

'Burning my hotel down?'

Her head jerked towards his again. '*Your* hotel?'

He stepped farther into the room, shrugged out of his jacket and placed it neatly on the hook by the door. 'You didn't like the decor?' he teased without answering her question.

She rolled her eyes. 'I was making dinner.' She eyed the bench in dismay. 'I don't know where I went wrong. I followed the recipe, but then I knocked the bowl, and while I was cleaning that up I neglected the oven and...' She shook her head. 'Stop smirking like that. I'll have you know I'm actually a halfway decent cook in my own kitchen. I just couldn't find anything and—'

'Decided dropping a bag of flour would help in some way?'

She laughed, tossing her head back so her blonde hair fluffed around her face. He stood very still, watching her, imprinting the view of her like this in his mind. It was somehow contrary to every preconception he had of Jemima Woodcroft.

'The flour had a mind of its own.'

'Ah.' He nodded sagely. 'I have heard of spontaneous grain combustion.'

'Right? It's totally a thing.'

'Naturally.' He grinned, holding a hand out to her. She moved around the bench after a slight hesitation, putting hers in his. She was so petite. He felt like a giant compared to her, so big, broad and oversized.

'I wanted to do something nice.' She grimaced.

The words held alarm. He didn't want 'nice'. That wasn't what this was about. He didn't particularly deserve nice, given that he'd blackmailed her into becoming his mistress. Worse than that, he'd lied about his level of interest in the hedge fund, intentionally concealing the fact he knew Laurence had inadvertently bought into the next big thing at ground level. 'Nice' didn't seem right.

'Why?'

She hadn't been expecting the question. Her face clouded with uncertainty. 'I don't know. I just thought…something different.'

He looked around the smoke-filled penthouse, quashing down the feelings her admission had aroused. He couldn't remember the last time someone other than a chef had cooked for him. Nor could he recall anyone, other than his mother, doing something 'nice' for him.

'We can't eat here,' he said after a moment. 'We'll go out.'

She looked over her shoulder. 'I guess we'll have to. Just give me a minute to clean.'

'Housekeeping will take care of it.' He squeezed her hand then dropped it, taking a step back, physically putting distance between them as emotionally he did the same. 'Let's go.'

The restaurant, right on the water, was one Jemima was familiar with. She'd come here several times, usually after a film festival event or following a shoot. It was the preferred haunt of models, actresses, billionaires—anyone who was anyone in Cannes came here to eat, drink, dance and be seen. Which meant there was a slew of paparazzi out the front, waiting for their next pay-cheque photo.

She was prepared for it, but still she stiffened for a moment as the lenses clicked and the flashes exploded. Her smile was instinctive, so too her body language. She had been in the industry long enough to know how to walk in such a way as to avoid giving an unflattering angle shot. Cesare, beside her, barely seemed to notice the photographers' attention.

Except, of course, he *had* noticed, as he did everything, and when they were seated a little while later he regarded her in that way he had, so watchful, so perceptive. 'You don't like being photographed.'

It wasn't a question. His observation sparked surprise inside her. 'I'm a model. It kind of goes with the territory.'

'I mean by paparazzi. You flinched outside.'

'No, I didn't.'

'I felt it. I saw it. No one else would have noticed, but I was right beside you, and I did. You don't like being photographed.'

'I don't like the paparazzi,' she corrected, reaching for her drink and taking a sip. 'I don't like being photographed when I'm doing something as mundane as walking or grocery shopping or going for dinner.' She lifted her shoulders. 'I don't like being chased through the streets when I'm going for a run or discovering my mail's been opened in the hope they'll find something scandalous. Do you know where one of those fake pregnancy stories came from?' she asked curtly, her lips compressed.

He shook his head a little, silently encouraging her to continue. 'I fell over and sprained my wrist. The doctor wanted to make sure there wasn't a break, so he sent me to get it X-rayed. At a place that also did ultrasounds. The invoice was sent to my home address, a nosy pap saw the name and the next thing I knew I was pregnant. With twins.' She rolled her eyes. 'So, yeah, it does make me a little wary, but I also understand it's just a part of my life.'

'I don't think people going through your mail should ever be a part of your life, irrespective of what you do for a living.'

'No,' she agreed, her anger simmering in her body. 'I hated that. To have your parents read that kind of story...' As if they hadn't already been through enough!

He was quiet for so long, she presumed he'd moved on. She turned her attention to the menu, reading it quietly, thinking ruefully of the badly burned dinner back at the hotel.

'Do you dislike it enough to change professions?'

She shook her head. 'I'm not sure I *could*

change professions. There's nothing else I'm trained for, and I don't know if there's anything else I'd be good at.'

'Your parents must have had misgivings about your chosen career?'

'I was fifteen,' she said with a terse shake of her head. 'They didn't really have much choice in the matter.' It was too much. She was betraying herself, her parents, the truth of her history. She pasted a bright smile on her face. She didn't want to talk to Cesare about her life. Not because it was secret but because it was sad and she didn't want to bring that into their evening.

'Anyway, I'm really fortunate. It's not an easy industry to survive in and I'm established enough now not to have to worry about my financial security. I'm pretty much guaranteed to get jobs and earn well.'

'Not that you need to,' he inserted silkily, and again she detected the faintest hint of mockery in the simple statement.

She kept her lips sealed. He obviously thought she was some incredibly wealthy heiress, and she couldn't really blame him for having formed that opinion. Her lineage was as it was, and Almer Hall was hardly the kind of house one owned without being wealthy enough to support it.

He could have no way of knowing how the inheritance tax had depleted her parents' capital—how Cameron's death had killed her father's career so that for a long time there was no money coming in and enormous bills piling up. He couldn't have known that the promise of lucrative modelling income was the only way a teenage Jemima could see of ensuring her parents—and she—kept the roof over their heads.

There was no trust fund waiting for her when she turned twenty-five. And despite her years of excellent earning, there was no safety net of savings for a rainy day. Laurence's hedge fund was the only hope she had that things would one day seem a little easier.

'What about you, Cesare?' She turned the conversation back to him as a way of preventing any more questions about her life and work. 'You could retire now and yet you don't.'

He laughed. 'Why would I retire?'

'You could afford to,' she pointed out.

'*Sì.*' He appeared to mull this over. 'But I would grow bored.'

'Surely you'd find a hobby?'

'A waste of time,' he said with clear condemnation.

'Why?'

'You think I should waste my time with—what?—orchid-growing? Golf? When I have the ability to do what I do?'

'I think there's more to life than work,' she said after a moment's consideration. 'Don't you?'

His shake of the head was slow and purposeful. 'That would depend on the individual.'

'And you don't want more than this.'

'Than what?' His watchfulness intensified.

'Than being a workaholic.'

'Is that what I am?'

She lifted a brow. 'You work seven days a week—unless you're just doing that now to avoid spending your days with me,' she added, a loop of uncertainty rocking her a little.

'No.' He shook his head. 'I haven't changed anything because of you.'

She was sure he didn't mean the words to be hurtful, but for some reason they were. It was simply further evidence of how little this relationship was going to impact him; how little it mattered.

'I work seven days a week, and have for as long as I can remember. I can't see that there's anything wrong with this.'

'You don't think?' She sipped her mineral water thoughtfully.

'You disagree?'

'Well...' Beneath the table, she crossed one leg over the other, unintentionally brushing his calf with the toe of her shoe. 'It doesn't seem like you have much...balance.'

'*Balance* is a fashionable word invented to give people a free pass to slack off.'

She stared at him, gobsmacked.

'Next you'll be suggesting I take up yoga.'

The idea was so ludicrous that she burst out laughing, shaking her head simultaneously. 'Actually,' she said when her laugh had subsided, 'Bikram is incredibly good for you. Relaxing, physically demanding, clarifying.'

'Perhaps you could show me,' he murmured, the words layered with sensual heat, so her insides squirmed and her breath grew shallow.

'Perhaps.' The word rushed out of her as images of his body, naked and contorting into whatever shape she wanted, filled her mind. She swallowed to clear her throat, but his eyes were teasing now and she flushed to the roots of her hair, the transparency of her thoughts something she wished she was better able to conceal from him.

'Don't you ever get lonely?' The question left her lips before she could analyse her reason for asking it.

'No.'

She contemplated that for a moment. 'I would. If I was you.'

'I like to be alone.' His voice had a rich, deep timbre. 'And when I want company, I find some.'

Jealousy tore through her. She blinked down at the table, surprised by the potency of her reaction. 'Of course.'

'I'm far more interested in how a woman like you lived a celibate life.'

Fortunately, a waiter's appearance saved her from answering. They placed their order and, by the time they were alone again, she was armed with another topic of conversation, something much more banal and light, something safely distanced from anything too personal.

It felt good to keep things on easy ground.

She liked talking to him, listening to him, and as long as they stayed away from anything to do with other lovers, or their personal lives, she could actually relax and enjoy the evening. It wasn't until they'd finished their coffees and *petits fours* that a sense of uneasiness crept back in.

'I'm serious, *uccellina*,' he murmured, and beneath the table his hand curved over her knee, so little darts of need immediately began to spiral through her. How much she wanted him was overwhelming—it was a physical need that seemed almost unconquerable.

Combined with the glass of wine she had enjoyed with her steak, it made her feel light-headed, buzzy and ready to succumb to her desire right then and there.

'What about?' The words were purred, kitten-like, and she had the satisfaction of seeing his eyes lower, sensual heat passing from him to her. She leaned forward a little, aware of the way her silk dress gaped at the cleavage, feeling his gaze drop there as though he were touching her.

'I am not a gambling man and yet I would

have bet my fortune on the fact you had the same kind of sexual experience as I have.'

'You were wrong.'

Bemusement crossed his features. 'Evidently. Why?'

There was no side-stepping this. 'There's no big reason.'

'I don't believe that.'

'Are you calling me a liar?' It was light-hearted, intended to take the conversation in a different direction, but if anything his look of concentration only deepened.

'You like to keep people at a distance,' he said after a moment, the shift in his questioning unexpected, and all the more so for how right he was. 'Whenever I ask you anything about your childhood, your work, your life, you shut me down. Why?'

She was tempted to deny it, but to what end? He was right. 'Does it matter?'

He frowned. 'Not particularly. I'm just curious as to why you would make a habit of closing people off.'

'I don't make a habit of closing *people* off...'

'Just me?'

She bit down on her lower lip, gnawing on

it thoughtfully. 'The parameters of this—' she pointed from her chest towards his '—were established at the beginning. Sex.' She dropped her gaze again. 'In exchange for your investment in Laurence's hedge fund.' Her stomach rolled with self-disgust. 'You didn't buy my inner secrets.'

'You don't think half a million pounds earns me a few secrets?' His tone was light, joking, but the words cut deep. It was her own fault for reminding him of the financial nature of this transaction.

Bitterness coated her insides.

'No.' She toyed with her napkin, wishing the conversation hadn't gone in this direction, wishing she didn't suddenly feel like this. 'There are some things even you can't buy.'

Thud. Thud. Thud. His feet; his heart. Cesare ran, and his body pumped; blood, muscles, legs, regrets.

When they'd returned to the penthouse the night before it had been immaculate once more, the smell of smoke dissipated, fresh flowers placed on the bench. They'd gone to bed and he'd made love to Jemima until dawn, delighting in the feel of her body even as something unpleasant was unfurling in his mind. It was a darkness he couldn't outrun, a presentiment of disaster he couldn't explain.

And then there was a darkness he could understand, one he had grappled with his whole life. Cesare Durante didn't like being told 'no'. He didn't like having his expectations confounded, nor did he like having to compromise.

True, this had begun as an exercise in sexual discovery. He'd wanted her physically and he hadn't much cared about anything else. But along the way the mysteries of Jemima had begun to unravel inside him, so that he needed neatly to tie them back together in order to be able to properly forget about her.

He needed to pull her apart, piece by piece, to understand her completely. Only then would he be able to walk away.

He needed her all to himself, and not just at night. They had four nights left of their agreed fortnight, and spending his days at the office no longer felt like a good use of that time. All his life, Cesare had been a person who did things properly, and he saw now that getting Jemima out of his system was going to involve more than sex. The things he didn't know about her made her all the more compelling, and the questions he had about her life filled him in a way only answers could relieve.

Without making a conscious decision, he turned around, moving back to the hotel. And as he went a plan firmed in his mind, a plan that would achieve his goals, a way to make it easier to walk away from Jemima at the end of this fortnight without a backward glance.

Relief flooded him, along with the certainty that this was the right decision, the sensible decision—the way to free himself of her magic once and for all.

CHAPTER TEN

ISOLA GIADA ROSE from the ocean like something from the prehistoric ages. Green all over, except for the strip of white sand that ran as a band around the island, and the turquoise water that lapped at its edges, it was breathtakingly beautiful.

'Just in case the airline, the hotel, the Alaskan hut and the hedge fund weren't enough?' she murmured, her eyes on his as he held a hand out to guide her from the speed boat that had brought them off the eastern coast of Italy.

'I wouldn't have thought someone like you would find that asset list surprising.'

'I think *anyone* would,' she corrected, his assumption about her wealth and background jarring. She dropped his hand as she surveyed the island some more. 'It's all yours?'

'Yes.'

'What else is there, beside this?'

She pointed a little way along the beach

where a stunning building seemed to lift from the sand itself, all white walls and glass. It was architectural and compelling while somehow also being organic and respectful of the environment.

'There are some small houses across the island—for staff, when I need them. On occasion, I have come here for weeks at a time, and generally have a housekeeper and the like to run things.'

'Naturally,' she murmured, his financial situation something she couldn't comprehend. She knew he was self-made, but it was almost impossible to fathom how anyone could build that kind of empire from nothing. 'Have you owned it long?'

Something shifted in his expression. 'Eleven years.'

Curiosity moved inside her. 'Did you build the house?'

'No.'

She gnawed on her lower lip thoughtfully. 'Why do I get the feeling there's a history here you're not sharing?'

He eyed her slowly, raking his gaze from the tip of her head to her toes, and at the same time a light breeze lifted off the ocean, so her loose dress pulled against her flesh, and she shivered for no reason she could think of.

'Because there is.' He held out his hand, and she put hers in it, just as she had the night before when he'd seen the disaster in the kitchen and drawn her from the midst of the mayhem.

'And you're not going to tell me?'

'That depends.' He lifted her hand to his lips, pressing a kiss to her inner wrist. A frisson of anticipation trembled across her spine.

'On what?'

'On what you're prepared to offer in exchange.'

Her heart skipped a beat. 'I don't get it.'

'Nothing is free, *uccellina*.'

He called her that often—little bird—but hearing it here, liberated in the Mediterranean, kissed by the sea air and the sunshine, did something strange to it, so that the moniker pierced the fabric of her being and became a part of her, as much as her eyes and her lips, her heart and her lungs. *Uccellina*.

He dropped his head closer, so his lips were just an inch from hers. 'I will answer any of your questions, if you answer all of mine.' His eyes were asking a billion questions of her and she felt stripped naked, raw beneath his scrutiny. And though it sparked a sort of anxiety inside her, there was also relief—a heady sense of calm that could only come with letting go.

Letting go of her barriers, letting go of their boundaries. Just for a moment, here in this slice of paradise far from the real world.

'Deal.' Her smile turned her eyes from emerald green to a sort of turquoise as vibrant as the ocean. They began to walk towards the house.

'Do you come here often?'

'Often enough.'

'I thought you were going to answer my questions.'

He stopped walking, tilting his face to hers, his eyes slightly mocking. 'By my count, you have left many of mine unanswered.'

'Oh. So I owe you?' she prompted, moving towards him with unconscious grace.

'Definitely.'

She grinned, pushing up onto the tips of her toes to lay a kiss against his lips.

'What do you want to know, then?'

'What do you think?' He held her tight, his body not relinquishing hers, and she felt it again—a loosening inside her, the usual restraint she held on herself sliding just a little. Enough.

The one question he'd asked repeatedly came to her—the pressing interest in how she had been a virgin the night they'd met.

'It's not like everyone thinks,' she said softly, making no attempt to move away from him. On the contrary—she liked being close to him like this; it made it easier to think and speak.

He was quiet, waiting for her to continue.

'Modelling.' She cleared her throat. 'It's exhausting and competitive and by the time I've finished a job the last thing I feel like doing is going out. Half the time, it's written into my contracts that I'll attend an after-party, like the other night—it helps with promotion, and apparently it's good for my image.' She couldn't help layering cynicism on the last few words. 'But I was young when I first started working,' she said wistfully. 'And far from home, and everything was…too much. Too loud and fast, and people were over-familiar, and I was… terrified, if I'm honest.'

She winced, hating how juvenile she sounded. 'I found that the louder it got, the busier, more hectic, the more successful I became and the more surrounded I was by other models and managers and photographers and social media managers and everyone, it just seemed to make me feel lonelier.'

'Your parents didn't travel with you?'

She compressed her lips. 'No.'

She was surprised he didn't push her for information—her response had been seething with words unspoken. But he let it go, and she was grateful for that.

'So you rejected the lifestyle completely and chose to live as a nun?'

She laughed softly, lifting a hand to his chest, her fingers splayed wide across his broad muscles, her nails painted a soft pink, her eyes transfixed by the sight for some reason. 'Pushing people away was a survival instinct and I never really stopped doing it.' She risked a glance at him and wished she hadn't when her heart skidded almost painfully against her ribs.

'And yet your image...' The words trailed off into nothingness. There was a look of uncomprehension on his handsome features, his lips tugged downwards, a frown on his face. 'If I didn't know beyond a shadow of a doubt that you were innocent, I would never have imagined the stories could be so wrong.' His hands lifted, as if of their own accord, to twist around some of her hair.

A troubled look crossed her features. 'I was sixteen when those stories began to run.' She dipped her face and then took a step away, turning to focus her gaze on the glistening ocean. It was stunning—like a mountain of turquoises had been dropped to float on top of the water's surface.

'It was said that you had a long-running affair with him—Clive Angmore.'

She nodded, the pain of that heavy inside of her. 'He was married.'

'But not faithful.'

She swallowed, nodding a little. 'No, he wasn't. His reputation bled into mine. I was *sixteen* when we met.' She shook her head with disapproval now. 'I'd been modelling for a year, but I was still so sheltered. I didn't realise what it meant when he started spending time with me, coming to my shows.'

Her eyes blinked shut at the memories—memories she tried not to think about. 'When he kissed me, it caught me completely off-guard. I'd never been kissed by anyone before and suddenly he was…' She lifted her fingers, brushing them over her lips as though she could erase the memory. She couldn't—it was a part of her, a part of her being, and that experience had built a layer of her armour, shielding her from future hurts.

'He was?' Cesare's voice held a tight restraint.

'He was on me.' Her throat was dry. 'He was heavy and strong—you know. He was older, but really fit. Anyway, I pushed him away, eventually, and he was furious—he was under the impression that I'd consented to being manhandled by him by virtue of the fact we'd eaten dinner together a few times.' Indignation made her voice wobble and she kept her gaze averted so she didn't see the way his hands were forming fists at his side, knuckles white in contrast to cheeks that were slashed with colour.

'I just thought he was taking an interest in my career.' She groaned, because she'd been so incredibly naive back then. 'I was lonely and he was nice. I thought he was…a friend.'

She heard Cesare's harsh exhalation, but didn't look at him. She couldn't. Her feelings were all stirred up inside her. 'I learned my lesson. People aren't just nice. Not without wanting something in exchange.'

Silence followed her pronouncement and, when she angled her face back to his, there was tension visible in his frame. A muscle jerked in his jaw. His eyes showed a hardness that sent a shiver down her spine.

'Anyway, by then the rumour mill was in full swing and no one seemed particularly interested in the truth.'

'So you stayed a part of that world, the same but different, always a little set apart from your friends.'

She nodded. 'It's not my real world,' she said simply. 'It's my job. It's work.'

'But you must have been curious?'

'About sex?'

'*Sì.*'

'I wasn't.' And then her eyes flitted to his. 'Until I met you, I'd never known anyone who made my world catch fire.'

She looked away again, the admission somehow making her feel vulnerable.

When he didn't speak, she moved to fill the silence. 'It's your turn.'

'For what?'

'To answer a question.'

'Fair enough. Ask away.' His voice was deep.

Her mind exploded with possibilities. There was so much about him she didn't know, and even though she'd sworn early on in this relationship that it would be safer *not* to know all his secrets, it was overwhelmingly vital now that she understood him.

'I don't know where to start,' she said simply, honestly.

When she blinked up at him, a smile had crossed his face. 'Come. Let me show you the house.'

At her sound of indignation, he laughed.

'I'll answer your questions—relax. We have four days. There is no rush.'

Only it felt as if there was. In the seclusion of the island time seemed both to stand still and move at warp speed, so two nights passed almost in the blink of an eye, every moment sublime. Swimming in the ocean, lying on the sunlit deck, a whole day spent in bed exploring one another, learning, needing, rewarding. She'd fallen asleep some time in the evening and woken up in the middle of the night, starving and full of desire all over again.

On the evening of the third night—their second last—they walked along the beach as the sun dipped into the ocean. It had been a perfect day. They'd explored the island, walking for miles until they'd arrived at a waterfall. They'd taken the steep rocky path to its bottom and swum in the creek at its base.

Jemima still didn't feel that she knew Cesare's secrets, but she knew *him*, all of him—his passion, his drive, his determination, his hunger. She understood him.

'It's so beautiful here.' She eyed the ocean. Despite the unendingness of it, she knew she would never tire of this view.

'Yes.'

'You're not tempted to live here permanently?'

'Sometimes.' But it was obvious from his tone that he was joking.

She mulled that over. 'Where *do* you live?'

He angled his head to face her, a grin on his face. 'I'm a citizen of the world.'

She couldn't help but return his smile. 'What does that even mean?'

'It means I fill my passport up every year.' He lifted his shoulders. 'I travel, a lot.'

'Sure, but you must have a home?'

'They're all my homes.'

She frowned. 'I don't think it works like that.'

His laugh was gruff and he stopped walking, pulling her into his arms and kissing her as though he simply couldn't help himself. 'Why not?'

But the kiss robbed her of breath and the ability to think, momentarily, so she had to concentrate to get her brain back into gear.

'Well, a home's a home. I think by its very definition it has to be where you spend the lion's share of your time. It's where you feel most comfortable, the place you crave when you want to just exist.'

Something flitted in the depths of his eyes, but then he kissed her once more and turned away, taking her hand in his and continuing their walk. 'Where's *your* home, then?'

'Almer Hall,' she responded without missing a beat. And because she knew and understood him on a soul-deep level, she sensed the tension that tightened his body even when she didn't comprehend the reason for it.

'You spend a lot of time there?'

'No.' Her smile was wistful. 'I have to live

in London, but I go back to Almer Hall when I can...' She bit down on her lip, aware she'd been about to say more than she wanted.

'But?' he prompted, his voice gravelly.

She looked up at him and something in the region of her heart panged. The sun was low behind his head, the sky a stunning shade of pink with streaks of purple cutting through from the horizon, but nothing was as breath-taking as Cesare Durante, and the full force of attention he was giving Jemima.

'It makes me sad too.' She shifted her head so she was looking straight ahead. It was easier to speak without looking directly at Cesare.

'Why should you feel sad?'

'That's a long story.' She tried to imbue her voice with light-heartedness and failed.

'And you don't want to tell it?'

She never really spoke about Cameron—not to anyone other than Laurence, anyway. It was hard. So hard to think of what they'd lost, of the life he should have been living. And yet, in that moment, on this secluded island, she *did* want to talk about him. To remember him and mourn him openly.

'I had a brother,' she said slowly, the words dragging across her heart.

Cesare didn't speak, and she was glad. She needed a moment to rally her thoughts and find her way to the words. 'Cameron. He was seven years older than me, so I grew up worshipping him, and he treated me like a pet.' Her smile was laced with that particular brand of happiness that reflected loss and remorse.

'He was kind to me and liked to make me laugh. I adored him, and for my parents… well…he was the second coming. The heir to the title, to Almer Hall, the first-born son of the first-born son of a first-born son.' She shook her head. 'You get the picture.'

'Yes.' The word was tight, forced from his lips.

'He died.' Tears filled her eyes; she didn't bother to push them away. 'I was six, and I didn't understand. One day he was there, and then he wasn't, and no one talked about it. My parents didn't know how to cope. They buried him without a funeral—it was just them and a priest at the family crypt. It was like he'd never existed. I couldn't understand it. It took me a long time to come to grips with what had happened.'

When she shifted her gaze to Cesare, he was watching her intently.

'He committed suicide. He was thirteen years old and he decided to end his life.' The words were raw, cut to shreds by the knives in her throat. 'He didn't leave a note or anything, but I caught up with some of his friends a long time afterwards. He was gay,' she said thickly. 'And he had no idea how my parents would react. He struggled for a long time, apparently, and just couldn't see a way past it.'

She swept her eyes shut and saw Cameron's beautiful, happy face. 'He was still a kid. Problems seem a lot bigger when you're young, and there was a lot of pressure on him. He grew up hearing about his legacy, his responsibility, the future of our family.' Jemima couldn't keep the disapproval from her voice. 'Such stupid notions in this day and age.'

Cesare stopped walking and Jemima did likewise, but she kept her face trained on the rocks in the distance.

'I wish I'd been older. I wish he'd trusted me enough to talk to me. I wish he'd known what an enormous hole he'd leave behind. I wish he knew how much I needed him, how much our parents loved him.'

Tears fell unchecked down her cheeks now.

'I'm sorry,' Cesare muttered, and because the words didn't seem sufficient, he pulled her into his arms, holding her tight to his body, his chin resting on top of her head. She stayed there, bundled against him, and breathed deeply, his masculine fragrance spreading along the rivers of her veins into every cell of her body. And despite the fact she'd carried this grief for almost two decades, it seemed to shift a little inside her now.

'I guess it's why I'm so close to Laurence,' she whispered. Cesare's hand, which had been stroking her back, stilled for a moment before continuing its reassuring journey. 'After Cam died, I was so alone. Mum and dad really went completely off the radar. It broke them. They blamed themselves; I see that now. I know they wish they'd done more, somehow made him see that they would love and accept him always.'

She swept her eyes shut. 'It was hard for them and they pushed me away. I guess I reminded them of him or something. I don't know. They were just destroyed by it. I spent a lot of time with my aunt after that, with Laurence. He was there for me when no one else was.' Her lips twisted into a melancholy grimace.

She pulled back a little so she could see his face properly. 'I came to dinner that night because he asked me to, and I'd do anything he needed.' And then a frown crossed her face and she lifted a finger to his lips to forestall a comment she anticipated he might make. 'But he never asked me to go home with you. That was all me.'

Something dark haunted his eyes. 'I'm truly sorry for what you went through.'

She nodded because there was nothing she could do but accept his words.

'I am surprised your parents were so liberal with you, after losing a child,' he murmured thoughtfully, as by silent consent they began to walk back towards the house. 'To allow you to become a model, without someone to go with you...'

'They checked out,' she said simply, and then found herself confiding the full story, even when it was something of which she *never* spoke, besides with Laurence. 'And we needed the money.' Her voice was thick with emotion. 'After Cam, Dad just…he couldn't function. He stopped working, so the repayments on Almer Hall got completely out of hand—the inheritance tax was pretty crippling even before— and we were in danger of losing the place. Mum and Dad parcelled off some of the land, but it barely made a dent.'

Cesare was looking directly ahead. 'And you use your modelling payments to keep them afloat?'

'I try to,' she confirmed. 'But it's exorbitant. They let the debt get way out of hand so there's millions of pounds in interest payments owing now. Honestly, there are times when I wish we would just sell it, but even if we did there'd still be money owing.'

He eyed her for a long time before nodding. 'And it's your home.'

'Yeah.' She blinked up at him and something twisted in her heart. 'It's my home.'

CHAPTER ELEVEN

'YOU GREW UP in the UK, didn't you?'

Beside her, Cesare pushed up onto his elbow, his eyes tracing her naked body with an insouciant possession that only served to fan the flames of her desire. They hadn't made it to the bedroom.

After their walk, they'd swum as the moon had breathed silver light across the ocean, their bodies seeking one another out in the inky water so that, by the time they'd returned to the house, they'd barely made it through the door before they'd been kissing, limbs entangled, hands moving quickly to disrobe each other of their underwear—not easy when they'd been saturated from the swim.

Lying now on the carpeted floor of the living room, Jemima felt heavy with desire, exhausted by the last few days but desperate not to sleep, not to express that she was tired.

They hadn't discussed it, but they both knew

what the morning would bring: their last day and night together.

'From when I was five.' He lifted a finger, tracing the outline of her nipple, drawing delicate circles over her pale pink flesh before he dropped his mouth to flick the same nipple with his tongue. Her body jerked in response and she shot him a look that was intended to serve as a warning but which instead spoke of hunger and flame.

'But you don't consider yourself to be British?'

He pulled a face. 'Definitely not.'

'But you lived there. Went to school there.'

'And left again as soon as I could.'

'Why?' His fingertips trailed down her body so lightly that she moaned and tried to lift up, to press against him and encourage him to touch her more, harder, to satisfy her all over again. His tight smile showed he understood, and it also showed the restraint he was using in not doing exactly that.

'I hated England with a passion.'

Her eyes jerked to his. 'Gee, thanks.'

His eyes sparked with hers, though with no apology in them. 'It's possible I resented being made to move there and that my resentment coloured everything that happened afterwards.'

'Why did you move?'

'My mother got a job.' It was a simple statement of fact and yet she felt a pull of curiosity, a feeling that he was only telling her part of the story.

'What does she do?'

'Did,' he corrected. 'She died, a long time ago. She was a nanny.'

Jemima reached for his hand, capturing it on her tummy and lifting it to her lips, pressing a kiss against his fingertips and holding it there as she pushed up onto her own side so she could see him properly, her body a mirror image of his.

'And she got a job working for someone in England?'

'Mmm.' He nodded crisply, his eyes glittering with a coldness that chilled her to the core. 'Gerald Montgomery White.' He said the name with abject disapproval.

She waited, watching him, curiosity expanding in her chest.

'You didn't like that?'

He was quiet for a long time, so she wondered if he was planning to ignore her, but then he expelled a long, gruff sigh. 'Not particularly.' He dropped his hand to her hip, tracing invisible circles there, his eyes transfixed by the gesture. 'She was a nanny, but they treated her like a slave. All her time was taken up by those children. And they were spoiled rotten, with a fog of entitlement trailing in their wake. I hated them.'

She grimaced. 'I've known people like that.'

'I'll bet you have,' he drawled.

'You thought *I* was like that,' she said, her eyes widening as comprehension dawned. 'When we first met! You were all things at dinner that night about where I grew up. You honestly thought I was one of those bratty kids, didn't you?'

His eyes probed hers and he nodded. 'Yes.'

She punched his arm, mock-playfully. 'Thanks a lot.'

'You had nannies growing up?'

'Yes.' Her expression softened as she thought of Cara. 'But she was like another mother to Cam and me.' And then, her heart shifted. 'She was fired, after Cam...' She shook her head to clear the memory, not wanting to go down that path. 'When did she pass away?'

'Almost twenty years ago,' he said. 'They didn't come to her funeral.'

'You wanted to keep it small?'

He shook his head. 'No. They were told of the date. None of them came. None of the children she raised—the children she raised while I was sent away to school.' His jaw tightened, his gaze awash with resentment. She lifted a hand to his chest, feeling the steady, deep beating of his heart with a rush of her own heartbeats. 'It was as though she didn't matter, like her life meant nothing.' His frown was deep, his expression so rich with feeling she found it hard to interpret his emotions.

She chose her words with care. 'That must have made it feel like she chose other children over you, and for nothing. I can imagine why you'd feel angry.'

His eyes slammed into hers, shock evident in their depths, as though he hadn't expected her to understand how he felt.

'Yes. It diminished her life. She deserved better.'

She nodded. 'You must have been hurt.'

'I was furious,' he muttered. 'I was sixteen years old and I'd spent six months preparing to lose my mother—she had cancer, terminal. But nothing prepares you for quite what that sense of being alone will feel like. It was the hardest day of my life, standing in the cemetery as her casket was lowered into the ground. That was the day I swore I would make the kind of money they took for granted.'

His features assumed a mask that was fearsome and compelling.

'I bought this island from a man named Ranulph Montgomery White—one of the boys she first looked after when we moved to England. He was a particularly nasty piece of work and seemed to delight in trying to make me miserable. I hated him and he hated me. So when this island came on the market...'

His smile was wolf-like.

'He'd developed a gambling addiction and needed the money. I drove the price down until it was a steal, and he was so desperate by then that he was practically begging me to go through with it. It's one of the most satisfying things I've ever done—sitting opposite a man who'd been a cruel, selfish bastard of a boy, who'd treated me and my mother as though we were nothing, and making him beg me to buy the place from him.'

Despite the chill that spread through her body, she couldn't help but feel a grudging sense of admiration at what he'd achieved, even if his motivations left a little to be desired.

'When I was sixteen, and I lost my mother, I swore I'd make her sacrifices count. And I have.'

'She would have been proud of you.' And then, with a flicker of a smile, 'Not for the maniacal revenge stuff, but for the incredible empire you've built. You are formidable and impressive.' She lifted a hand to his cheek, holding his face steady. 'She would have been proud of you, but I'm sure she was anyway.'

His eyes clung to hers, as though he couldn't pull them away, and she felt the same, her gaze locked to his.

'I've never known anyone like you,' she whispered, wondering at the heaviness that accompanied that admission.

'No?'

'Your determination is…remarkable.'

'You've said that already.' He brushed his lips over hers.

'Then I guess that makes you doubly remarkable.'

She felt his smile against her lips.

'I can't imagine how you did all this.'

'I worked hard.'

'Still…to build this from nothing…'

He lifted his head so she could see the strength in his gaze. 'When I want something, I get it. Not because I am lucky or charmed, but because I move the pieces around until I'm guaranteed to win.'

His words took half her breath away; his kiss finished the job.

It was past midnight. Not far past, somewhere in the small hours of the morning. Cesare presumed Jemima was sleeping. Her breathing was even, her body still. He lay on his back, his head tilted towards her, his eyes resting on her frame out of habit, so when she shifted, rolling slowly to face him, he was surprised.

'You were asleep.'

'Dozing,' she corrected, lifting her fingertip

to his lips and tracing the outline slowly, her eyes following the gesture.

'Ah. Same thing?'

'No.' She shook her head, and there was something in her gaze that spoke of trouble and worry. 'I was thinking.'

'Ah. About?'

'The night we met.' She dropped her finger to his chest, spreading her palm over his pectoral muscles, a faraway look in her eyes. 'If you thought I was just a snob, like the kind of kid your mother looked after, why did you kiss me?'

He frowned. The question was valid—it was one he'd asked himself often enough. 'I wanted you.'

She pulled a face. 'Sure. But you're not someone who reacts to his every whim. You're disciplined and determined and a workaholic. No way would you have taken me home with you on a whim.'

His frown deepened, because her assessment was accurate and it filled him with a sense of impatience. 'You were there, and I presumed quite willing to offer yourself to me to make things go more smoothly with your cousin.'

He saw the fierce look of rejection fire in her gaze and wanted to ease it.

'I was wrong.'

Her expression shifted, but her eyes dipped down, away from his gaze, so he couldn't fathom what she was thinking. 'Yes. This was never about Laurence.'

He found himself wishing that were the truth, wishing she hadn't been motivated in part by a loyalty to her cousin.

'Not that night, no.'

'Not any of it.' Her eyes bounced back to his.

'This fortnight,' he reminded her, 'came about because of your need for me to invest in his hedge fund.'

She frantically massaged her lip from side to side. 'It's why I went to see you, but not why I agreed to this.' Her throat shifted as she swallowed. 'I need you to know that before—before tomorrow and before I…we… Before this ends.' She dropped her hand and her face was tight, her features taut. 'I don't want you to look back on this and rewrite what we were.'

Something stone-like rolled through his gut. Visceral disagreement. He wasn't going to look back on his time with Jemima. He never thought of past lovers. It wasn't in his genetic coding. And Jemima would fall into that same category once this was over.

He made the promise to himself, but it lacked true conviction. There was a part of him that loathed the fact their agreed time was coming to an end. A fortnight had seemed over-generous, initially—when had he ever wanted a woman for so long?—but he struggled now to imagine her body being denied to him. And her laugh. Her smile. Her kindness.

He closed his thoughts down with the sheer force of his willpower.

It was irrelevant. They had a deal and he intended to uphold his end of it.

'I won't.'

'I'm not here for Laurence.' She pierced him with her bright green gaze then, and he found it hard not to pull her to him, not to kiss her so that she smiled and sighed against him, her body soft and pliant.

'Then why did you agree to this?'

'Honestly?'

'That's what we said, isn't it?'

Her nod was just a slow lift of her head. 'I

wanted you. I hadn't been able to stop thinking about you.'

His eyes swept shut for a moment, and he hated how delirious her admission made him feel. It was the exact opposite of what he wanted. He hadn't come into this expecting to *feel* anything. It was sex—lots of sex, great sex—with a woman who meant nothing to him. More than that, she was exactly the kind of woman he wouldn't usually touch with a ten-foot pole—her aristocratic roots were a permanent mark against her.

But she was nothing like he'd expected, nothing like her reputation suggested and nothing like he presumed her upbringing would have made her. She was just Jemima. Sweet, kind and utterly compelling.

'Yes, I was desperate for you to buy into the hedge fund. And I'm so glad you did. I couldn't bear to see Laurence fail and hopefully, if the market goes well, he'll be able to help with Almer Hall soon, to take some of the pressure off me.' Her smile reached deep inside him and yanked at his heart. 'But I never would have agreed to sleep with you again, no matter the price, if it wasn't what I really wanted.'

There was danger in her promise, danger because it suggested she was offering something he had intentionally avoided all his life. Acceptance. Affection.

He was glad their time together was almost over, glad their clean break was at hand. Glad he could go back to the way things had been before this.

Except, he wasn't.

He thought of that future, he thought of not seeing her again, and something like a blade pressed against his chest, making breathing something of which he was painfully aware.

He turned his face away from her for a moment, a frown etched across his features as he studied the view from the window. There wasn't much to see—just the dark ocean with a single, shimmering triangle of moonlight right at its centre.

'So if I cancelled my investment now you wouldn't mind?'

He felt the movement of the bed as she shifted a little. 'Of course I would. But not because I've been here for a fortnight, and this relationship was predicated on that, and you'd be breaking your word or whatever. I'd mind because you made a promise to Laurence and he's counting on you. I'd mind because it would be a terrible thing to do.'

He turned back to face her and spoke softly, wanting to erase the little line of worry that had formed around her eyes. 'Relax. I have no intention of doing any such thing. But you are naive if you don't see how connected my investment is with your decision to become my mistress.'

'I…didn't say they weren't connected.'

'I propositioned you because I desired you, and because I knew that desire to be mutual. But you agreed because you couldn't not.' Her face paled beneath his scrutiny. 'I told you, I'm good at this. I manoeuvre all the pieces until I get what I want. It's not luck. It's not chance. It's how I work.'

It was dark in the room, only the brief glint of moonlight to provide any illumination, but he saw the hint of tears on her lashes. 'You're wrong,' she whispered. 'That's not why I'm here.'

Rejection fired through him, but he softened his tone, speaking calmly, gently, with only the slightest undercurrent of iron. 'Yes, it is.

And that's okay. We all have our price—at least yours was charged in the service of something noble.'

His words were still ringing in his own ears in the morning; he hated to think of how she must feel, of how she was remembering what he'd said. They hadn't spoken again since. She'd turned her back on him and silence had fallen, so it had been impossible to push those words from his mind, impossible to forget how he'd felt and why he'd said that.

But as night gave way to dawn, and she continued to sleep beside him, he pushed carefully out of bed. It was their last day together, their last night, and the thought gave him no pleasure.

He wasn't ready to let her go.

It was the one thing he was certain of. The night before, he'd told himself it would be a relief to end this, but that had been a lie.

She was a distraction he didn't want, but her ability to commandeer his thoughts wouldn't disappear when she did.

He had set out to get her out of his head once and for all, but he hadn't achieved that—yet.

He needed more time. More nights and days to let his fascination burn out. He needed to forget her and move on, and then he could go back to being his old self.

Cesare strode from his room, barefoot and naked, pausing to grab a towel from behind the door as he went, which he slung low on his hips as he made his way to his office.

There, he set to work, moving the pieces into position, finding the information he needed, doing everything he could to ensure he would, as before, get the same answer from Jemima that he needed.

Bending people to his will was Cesare's gift, and he intended to utilise it again this morning. The machinations were beneath him, of that he had little doubt, but—more than ever before—the ends would justify the means. He was sure of it.

CHAPTER TWELVE

SHE SLEPT LATE, which was little wonder, given how long she'd stared at the wall of his bedroom the night before, her mind sagging under the weight of his words, his statement filling her with a sense of disbelief she couldn't shake.

We all have our price—at least yours was charged in the service of something noble.

It wasn't true.

Anxiety for Laurence had brought her to Cesare, but nothing that had happened between them was because of her cousin, or his financial predicament. She wasn't mercenary and her body sure as hell wasn't for sale. This had been about temptation, lust nnd desire.

Her stomach squeezed and her heart did the same, twisting inside her, so she made a little gasping noise and pushed back the duvet, looking around for her phone. It was charging, across the room. She strode towards it and checked the time—after ten. She took her time going downstairs, showering and dressing in a pair of white linen shorts and a silk halter-neck top that she'd modelled in Paris earlier in the summer.

Barefoot, she made her way through the house, unintentionally quiet, as though she didn't want to see Cesare. As though she wouldn't know what to say to him when she did.

It was another stunning day. Bright blue sky, turquoise water, sand that she knew from experience would be soft and spongy beneath her feet. She pressed a button on the coffee machine, her eyes fixed to the view, her body awash with feelings she couldn't process.

This would be her last day with Cesare. She'd prepared for that. From the beginning, she'd known this would end, and she'd made her peace with it. But even after the night before, after what he'd boiled their relationship down to, the accusation that she was so mercenary, she felt an agonising ache when she thought of leaving him.

The coffee machine was silent but efficient. She reached for the cup and pulled it from the machine, lifting the fragranced drink to her nose first, breathing in the comforting aroma before taking a sip, her eyes fluttering shut.

But the second she closed them she saw Cesare. All facets of him, every side that she'd seen over the past two weeks and on their first night together, and her tummy rolled with uncertainty. Doubts and disbelief crowded through her.

This couldn't really be the end, could it?

She tried to imagine her life back in London. Going away on assignment, taking part in that world which now seemed even more superficial than usual, travelling home to Almer Hall and feeling her parents' loneliness, their grief, and knowing that she carried something within her that would eclipse it.

Life without Cesare.

She couldn't think that thought through any further. Cesare entered the kitchen at that moment, his footsteps breaking through Jemima's concentration, and she turned her head to the side, not quite able to meet his eyes.

'Morning.'

His silence had her moving her body to look at him properly, and there was an expression on his face she didn't recognise. He was serious, his features held in a mask of indifference, but his eyes—eyes that she could now read like a book—spoke of something bigger. Something important.

'You're awake.'

She nodded, even though it was more a statement than a question.

'Good. We need to talk.'

She curved her hands around her coffee cup to stop them from shaking and waited, her bottom propped against the kitchen bench. He came to stand opposite her, his frame deceptively relaxed.

'I don't want this to be our last day together.'

She wasn't sure she'd heard him properly.

'What?'

She didn't trust herself to say more than that. Just a small noise, urging him to continue.

He crossed his arms over his chest. 'I don't know how long this will last. I don't have the answers I thought I did. You've surprised me. But I know I don't want this to end.'

Relief began to shift inside her. 'I don't, either.'

'I know.'

His arrogance would have been galling if it wasn't so completely his trademark.

A smile lifted her lips.

'I can't take any more time off work. For this to work, we'd need to be based in Rome. If you wished to take on assignments, you could use my jet for as long as we continue this arrangement.'

Alarm bells began to tremor, just a little. She lifted her eyes to his, confusion marching across her face. 'What arrangement?'

'You being my mistress.'

And just like that, as if a pin had been slipped into a balloon, her happiness burst. She stared at him, non-comprehending. 'Your mistress?' she croaked after a moment.

He nodded, reaching for her, and she was so shocked that she didn't resist at first. She let him draw her gently towards him, her coffee between them, his body so familiar to her, so perfectly matched; he was everything she wanted.

'It would be more of this, more of what we've shared these last two weeks, until we're ready to move on.'

It was as though she were being pushed towards a cliff in a little buggy over which she had no control. His words were so calm, so ordered, and he spoke with the total authority of a man who had made a plan and expected it to be adhered to. But the last part of his calmly delivered directive rocked her to the core of her being.

Ready to move on.

Her insides began to fill with heat, as though lava were being poured through her body, and she shook her head urgently, pulling away from him, sipping her coffee then placing the cup down so she could dig her hands into the pockets of her shorts.

'We can put a time limit on it again, if that helps,' he murmured, standing exactly where he was, watching her with eyes that saw too much. 'A month?'

Her eyes swept shut as disbelief spun through her. 'A month,' she repeated, nodding a little, even though she had no intention of going along with it. Disbelief was running rampant through her.

A month.

It wasn't enough. It would never be enough. Her lungs seemed to be squeezing shut; she couldn't get enough air. She bit down on her lip and tried to stay focussed; she tried not to let herself give in to the tears that were threatening to fill her eyes.

'I can help you with Almer Hall.'

Her eyes burst open and tore to him. He was watching her, completely still, his body unmoving.

'What?'

'I want to help you,' he said, but it was as though the words were being torn from him against his will.

'Help me how?'

'There are four mortgages against the title.' Now he moved, walking towards her, his eyes holding the slightest recrimination. 'You've been chipping away at them, but not in a way that will make any real dent.'

A sense of defeat made her defensive. 'How do you even know that? It's private.'

'I have ties at your bank.'

'Jesus.' She shook her head in disbelief. 'And they, what—handed over confidential financial information?'

'This information is not confidential—just difficult to obtain unless you know what you're doing. And I do know what I'm doing, Jemima. I want to help you with Almer Hall.'

And then, comprehension dawned. A wave of nausea crested inside her as she tumbled over that cliff, the little buggy she was in not equal to the pressure being exerted on it any longer.

Grateful for the wall at her back, she used it for support, staring at him for several long seconds. Had she misunderstood?

We all have our price—at least yours was charged in the service of something noble.

That was what he truly thought of her. She blinked, and for a second she felt a rush of hatred for him. Hatred that was all the more intense for the fact she didn't hate him at all and her heart knew that. Her heart knew why this hurt her so badly, why after everything she'd been through, why a woman who had—as he'd said—become adept at pushing people away, should feel his insult at the very centre of her being.

'You're saying you'll help me. But only if I accept this…proposition?'

His eyes flared with something she didn't comprehend.

'I'm offering to give you everything you

could ever want,' he said simply, neatly avoiding having to answer the accusation she'd laid at his feet.

But he was so wrong! Wrong in every way.

'No.' A whisper. 'You only think you are.'

His finger pressed to her chin, lifting her face to his, his eyes probing hers. His question was raw, though, his words dragged from deep within him. 'Are you saying you want this to be the end? That you would wish to stick to the original terms of our agreement?'

She could fight the tears no longer. They filled her eyes, and she shook her head, knowing her voice would tremble if she tried to speak.

Relief crossed his features, followed closely by triumph. 'And nor do I. This is the solution.' He took her silence for tacit approval. 'Come to Rome with me for one month. You will have everything provided, but most of all I will clear Almer Hall of all debts. One month as my mistress and you can spend the rest of your life knowing your family's home is safe, that your parents can live without worry.'

A sob filled her lungs. She swallowed it away. 'Just like you said?'

'What do you mean?'

'Everyone has their price?'

For the smallest sliver of time, she saw remorse glimmer in the depths of his eyes, but then it was gone, arrogance replacing it. 'It was not intended as an insult.'

She made a snorting noise then, shaking her head. 'You don't think?'

'I wasn't speaking specifically about you—this could apply to anyone.'

'I don't believe that.'

'Believe it or not, it's the way the world works. I'm not saying Almer Hall is the only reason you'll agree to this, but I know that it makes it easier for you to say yes to what I'm offering.'

'You're wrong,' she insisted. 'The terms you've laid out make it harder. If you'd asked me to stay with you longer purely because you don't want me to go, because you can't bear to wake up tomorrow without me in your bed and in your life, then I would have said yes a thousand times over. But to agree to be your mistress on the same mercenary terms as before—after everything we've shared—how can you think me capable of that?'

His eyes shifted with something dark.

'Why do you want me to stay?' she demanded, unable to believe the worst of him, even with all the evidence at her feet.

A muscle jerked in his jaw, as though he were clenching his teeth.

'Tell me.'

He was silent.

'Say it. I need to understand what's brought you to this point. I need to know what you feel.'

'What I feel?' Finally he spoke, the words bursting from him, showing his frustration and impatience. 'I don't know. I've never done this before. I presumed two weeks with you would be enough, and it hasn't been. I know I'll get over this—that I'll get over you—but I need more time. I need more of you.'

'Wow.' She swept her eyes shut for a second. 'I've never heard myself talked about as though I were a narcotic before.'

He grimaced. 'I only meant—'

'That you're not over me. That you want me in your life until it suits you for me to leave, and not a moment beyond that. And what about me, Cesare?'

'I told you, you'd have everything you could ever want.'

'What if all I want is you?'

He looked confused, as though such an idea had never occurred to him.

'You'd have me. Every night, just like you have this last couple of weeks.'

'No.' She shook her head with urgency. 'That's not what I mean.'

'Well, what *do* you mean? What do you want? I will give you anything if you'll agree to this.'

His words pulled at something inside her, something that forced her to dig deep and really see what she'd perhaps known all along. His offer should have been tempting, on some level. More of Cesare? Even one more month, knowing the end would come, was still *something*. But she knew each day would be agony, that to accept his terms with the knowledge he intended to end it would be a form of barbarous torture.

She straightened, moving away from the wall, pacing towards the windows that framed the spectacular view of the ocean.

'Meaning what, exactly?' Her voice was hoarse, her tender heart trying to come to grips with the realisations that were exploding through her.

'Almer Hall will be unencumbered. All you have to do is say the word.'

'And you'll call my bank and pay millions more pounds, just so I'll make love to you until you decide you don't want me?' She whirled around, grabbing onto her fury with both hands, glad to have it, infinitely glad to feel it, needing its barren echo to rattle her into sense. 'And if I want more? Credit cards? Dresses? Diamonds?'

His eyes widened for a moment and then he shrugged, his expression so loaded with determination that her heart swelled in pain for him. How little did he value himself to think such luxuries would ever be necessary?

'If you wish.'

'No, damn it!' She waved her hand through the air emphatically and his eyes followed the gesture, watching her in the way he had that was so intense it was like a caress.

'Damn it.' She groaned again. 'Do you really think I want *any* of that?'

'You have told me how much Almer Hall means to you,' he said quietly.

'I know!' Fury eclipsed everything else. She spun away from him, staring at the ocean, its endless rolling towards the shore something from which she would ordinarily have taken reassurance. But she didn't. Not then. She couldn't.

'And that you would use that knowledge to blackmail…after everything…'

'It's not blackmail,' he denied. 'This is me giving you what you want, and us both getting what I think we need: more time together.'

'And if I let you do this, you'd be proved right in what you said last night, and I will never let you think me capable of that.'

She wasn't looking at him, so didn't see the surprise that crossed his features.

'This wasn't about the hedge fund for me, Cesare. I meant that. I simply wanted to be with you, and I still do.'

His exhalation of breath spoke of relief, but she whirled around to look at him then, grief in every line of her body.

'But you'll never give me what I really want, and spending another night with you, knowing what your limits are, knowing what you think of me…' Her voice cracked and she had to pause to take a breath and calm her breaking heart. 'It's not possible. It would be hell on earth.'

But he wasn't ready to let this go. 'I've just told you I will give you anything.'

'Not this.'

'What? What do you want?' He moved towards her, and she flinched, not out of fear of him so much as a fear of how readily she could weaken and give in, just to have more time with him. That alone was a reason to stand firm, to hold her ground, because it would destroy her to spend more time with him under these conditions.

'I want more.'

'Sì, uccellina.'

His eyes scanned her face and her heart turned over because she truly believed that, in that moment, he would have acceded to whatever demand of him she wished to make. So long as it was within his financial means, at least.

She lifted a hand to her chest, her features showing heartbreak. 'I want this to be real.' She felt his chest tighten. Her voice was hoarse with unshed tears. 'I want to wake up beside you without the phantom ticking of a time bomb as the end draws nearer. I want to wake up beside you every morning for the rest of our lives.' She swallowed, shocked at how important it felt to say this, even as she saw disbelief etch itself across his face. 'I want you to love me like I love you,' she whispered, and even then she hoped. She hoped when there was no reason to because that was the transformative power love held.

She stared at him, her breath held, her eyes huge, and she waited.

And finally he said what she'd known he would. That didn't stop it from hurting, though.

'It's not possible.'

'Why not?' she challenged, her eyes determined even as they filled with tears.

He stayed perfectly still, except for nostrils which flared as he exhaled through them, slowly, as if he was trying to calm his temper. 'I am offering you something very clear. The same thing I've offered all along. Sex. Fun. Full stop.'

'No.' She denied this. 'You really think that's what we've been doing?'

At least he had the decency not to rush into agreement. 'There are limits to this. Limits to the time we will spend together, limits to what I can offer you. There are boundaries and rules, and that's good for both of us.'

'Not for me,' she returned insistently. 'I don't want boundaries with you. I want to tear them down and revel in all of you, all the time.' She lifted up onto the tips of her toes, so her lips were only an inch or so from his. 'Tell me you don't feel the same way.'

He didn't move, and her heart slammed into her ribs and desperate hope overtook her every nerve ending.

'When my mother died, I swore I would earn my fortune. I swore I would devote my life to that, to making something of myself. It is the only thing I have ever wanted, Jemima. Relationships aren't a part of who I am. I made this decision a long time ago, and nothing— no one—will change my mind.' He lifted his hands to cup her face then, holding her right where she was, so his eyes could devour every detail of her features. 'You are not like any woman I have ever known, and if I was ever going to put that rule aside it would be for you.' He padded his thumb over her lip. 'But it's not what I want.'

'*I'm* not what you want,' she corrected.

'I do,' he corrected. 'I want you, just not in that way.' She sucked in a harsh breath that spoke of her pain, but he continued regardless. 'I want what we have now. I want it for a little while longer, and then I want us to look one another in the eyes, to smile and to say good-bye and thank you, knowing we will never see each other again, but that these memories will always be with us. Can't you see how right that is? How good?'

Her chest ached. 'Leaving you will never feel right. Now, or in a month—never. I'm in love with you, Cesare. There's no sense, no reason, no sensible, calm, rational end-point to this for me. I love you. I want to spend my life with you. I want to, I don't know, have a family with you.' The words weren't planned, but as soon as she said them they felt completely true in her soul. 'I want to grow old with you at my side. I just want you.'

His expression was laced with shock. 'This has *never* been on my radar.'

She swept her eyes shut. 'I didn't know it was on mine until a moment ago. But I do know it, Cesare. In every bone in my body, I know how I feel, and I know that I love you and that I can't stay with you another moment if there's no hope that you might love me back.'

'There's not.' The words cracked around her. 'Listen to me.' His voice was gentler then, an attempt to soften the sticks of dynamite he'd thrown into the room. 'You don't love me. It's completely understandable that you do, but that's just your inexperience showing. You love sex.' His lips twisted in something like amusement and her fingertips ached to slap him.

'How dare you?' She shook her head. 'Don't diminish what I feel. I know the difference between lust and love.'

'Do you? How?'

Her temper spiked. 'Lust is what I felt for you that night in London, when you kissed me in the restaurant, when you took my virginity. Lust is what I felt when you made my body yours, when you filled me with desire for the first time. Love is what I felt when you showed me what's in here.' She pushed at his chest. 'When you talked about your mother and your childhood and your business and your life. Love is what I felt when you asked me about *my* life, when you saw beyond the fact I'm Jemima

Woodcroft and wanted to know what made me tick. Love is what I felt, night after night, as you held me in your arms and kissed me with a gentleness that came from deep within your soul.'

His features were like ice. 'Jemima...' She waited for him to speak, but he said nothing. He simply stared at her for so long that her lungs hurt, because she was holding her breath and waiting, needing him to say something that would make all this better.

'I think you love me, too,' she whispered, and she felt as though she were stepping so far out on a limb that it was creaking audibly. 'You keep saying I'm different from any woman you've ever known. You spent half a billion pounds to get me into bed and you want me to stay another month. How do you know that will be enough? How do you know we won't be having this same conversation in a month's time?'

'Because I have decided what I want, and I'll stick to it this time.'

She shook her head, sorrow for him rippling through her soul. 'You can't just switch your feelings off like that, Cesare. You want me in your life, and you know you do.' She couldn't let this go. She needed him to see that they were both in love. 'You spent half a billion pounds because you couldn't risk that I'd say no to you.'

His eyes swirled with darkness and he took a step back from her, his face angular, his look somehow distant. 'I had already ordered my lawyers to buy into the hedge fund. Getting you in bed was just the cherry on top.'

His words made no sense. She shook her head, disputing them. 'No, you hadn't. You told me you wouldn't, remember? Unless I came away with you.'

'I lied.' His eyes glowed when they met hers. 'I lied to get what I wanted—you. I leveraged what I could, knowing that you would do any-thing for your cousin.'

She gaped, none of it making sense.

'This is the man you think you love. This is what I'm capable of.'

She lifted her fingers to her lips, shaking her head. 'But why?'

'Because I couldn't risk that you wouldn't agree. Not because I love you, but because I wanted you, and I succeed at all costs, always.'

She ignored his admission and the wounds it

inflicted. 'I mean, why did you buy such a huge share of the hedge fund? I know it wasn't altruism. And if it wasn't for me, then what was it?'

He shifted his eyes above her head for a moment then pinned her with a steely glance. 'Your cousin is sitting on a gold mine and he doesn't yet realise it. The five hundred million pounds I spent will be worth a billion by the end of the year, easily.'

Her knees felt weak. 'What?' It was hoarse. Soft. So soft it was almost inaudible, but he heard because he replied.

'When it comes to business, if not people, I do my research. I knew what he had that night in the restaurant. You were always just a silver lining to that deal. I don't let business and pleasure get mixed up.'

She closed her eyes, wanting to blot out the world, but he was relentless.

'See? You do not love me, right? How could you?'

Her heart splintered for him because she saw the truth so clearly now—the little boy who'd grown into a man who believed all he had to offer was money. Who believed that maybe his mother would have loved him more if she could have seen the wealth he'd amassed. A man who ended things with women before they could walk out on him.

'In spite of this, I love you. In spite of the fact I am hurt, and feel betrayed and used and cheap, I still love you.' She bit down on her lip, the truth of her words etching into her. Saying it was so liberating, so freeing.

'And yet you knew I would never love you back.'

'No,' she whispered, her eyes haunted.

'Yes. I have told you exactly what kind of man I am, what I'm capable of, and you ignored that.'

'You're wrong. I know what you've said about yourself, but I see you as you really are. I see someone you don't even know is there.' She lifted her chin defiantly, her body tense with pride even when her heart was in shreds.

But he shook his head, denying that. 'You only think you do.'

'Cesare…' She sighed softly. 'You've spent a lifetime trying to outrun your roots. You think that if you work harder, make more money, fill your bank account, your asset list or whatever, that you'll finally feel okay? That you'll feel whole?'

She stared him down and saw the shift in his expression, the hardening in his eyes, and she knew he wasn't going to listen to her, that no matter what she said he was determined to stay the course.

'Why did you get your tattoo?' she pushed. *'Come sono*—"as I am".' His surprise was obvious. 'You are as you are and I love you as you are.' She waved a hand around the magnificent beach house. 'None of this matters to me. There's an inherent value in *you*, just you, and I see it even if you don't.'

A muscle jerked in his jaw. 'You're wrong about me.'

'No, I'm not. You're a good man—'

'I mean you're wrong to think I'm broken in some way, or that I don't feel whole. I live my life the way I choose. I do what I want.'

'And that's not me.'

He swept his eyes shut.

'I don't mean for a month,' she added quickly. 'I mean for ever.'

He fixed her with a cool gaze, as though this were easy for him. 'No, Jemima. I could lie to you right now and pretend, just to get more time with you, but I won't do that. This is what I'm offering—the decision is yours.'

She nodded, anguish making her face pale.

'It's not a decision,' she whispered. 'I have to go. I can't stay.'

Neither of them moved or spoke for several seconds, and then she said again more urgently, because she felt as though she were suffocating, 'I have to go, Cesare, please.'

But he shook his head, disbelief etched in his features. 'No.'

Her laugh was dry, lacking any humour. 'You just said it was my decision.'

'Stay a week,' he implored, his voice thick. 'Same terms. All your debts disappear.'

She sobbed. 'Don't.' She lifted a finger to his lips. 'You aren't this man.'

He stared into her eyes.

'You aren't this man, and I'm not that woman,' she insisted. 'You're so much better than this.'

CHAPTER THIRTEEN

HE WAS CONSCIOUS of the date from the moment he opened his eyes. Four weeks to the day after Jemima had walked out of his life, he woke to the realisation this should have been the day they ended it. If she'd agreed to his proposition, then they'd have been together this whole time.

Instead, he'd acceded to her wishes, knowing it was the right thing to do even when every fibre of his being had wanted to insist she finish the fortnight, just as she'd promised; that she give him one more night. Instead, he'd flown her by helicopter to the mainland and had his jet fuelled up to take her back to England. He hadn't travelled with her. It would have felt like prolonging the inevitable.

Besides, she'd barely been able to look at him at the end.

So much for love.

Was it love that could make you push someone away like this?

He stared out at the lake, still as anything, with a mystical layer of fog hovering just above the water on this cool early autumnal morning, a scowl on his face as he relived every moment of that last day. Her face pinched and uncertain, her eyes so filled with hurt and disappointment, and worst of all, his inability to say or do anything to fix it.

For the first time in his adult life, Cesare Durante had been without adequate words. He'd wanted to reassure her even when he knew he couldn't—because what could he offer her? Not love.

And that was all she'd wanted. She'd been very clear.

With a sound of frustration, he pushed up from the deck chair, moving into the old log cabin. The morning was cool, but he wore low-riding jeans. No top. He liked the cold. He was glad of it. Glad of the rush it gave his blood, as well as the feeling of being alive, alive in a way he seemed to crave these days.

He made a coffee, thick and black, and poured it into one of the enamel cups his Alaskan cabin had come furnished with.

He drank it quickly, then turned his gaze back to the lake.

He needed to run. To run faster than he had the day before. He hadn't been able to outrun his thoughts then, but maybe today? Pausing only to pull on a crisp white shirt and a pair of joggers, he shouldered out of the door and set off around the lake.

He couldn't outrun her. She was a fog in his brain, filling his mind, taking over his every thought. Except it wasn't her. It wasn't Jemima so much as the fact he knew how wrong he'd been, and he hated that. He hated knowing he'd been at fault, and worse that he'd hurt her. He'd lied to her to get her to agree to be his mistress. He'd blackmailed her with her cousin's future and wellbeing. Then he'd tried to blackmail her all over again, just for good measure.

His behaviour had been deplorable.

He growled and ran faster...*thud, thud, thud.* A twig cracked beneath his foot. He kept running, his head bent low. He ran and he ran and he didn't look where he was going so that he was almost on top of the grizzly bear when he saw it.

He froze, his pulse firing up a notch, his instincts kicking in. Adrenalin sent a metallic taste into his mouth and his eyes flew wide. The bear was eating a fish, ripping it in half, but as Cesare stood there the grizzly turned its formidable head, its dark-brown eyes turning to study him.

He was metres away from a beast that was more than capable of ripping him to shreds. He should run. Retreat. Do something. Anything.

Save himself.

He didn't. He stared at the bear, his expression grim, and not particularly sure he cared what the hell happened to his pathetic excuse for a life. He stared at the bear and saw himself, saw himself clearly. He saw the path he was on, the life he was willingly choosing, and he almost willed the bear to come at him.

Because there was surely no point to life if you lived it as he did?

The thought was brief and fleeting and completely startling. He stared at the bear, the bear stared back and then, remarkably, it shrugged its shoulders, turned and began to thump heavily away in the opposite direction.

Cesare stood perfectly still, watching the bear

go, no longer willing to be his quarry. He stared at the bear's retreat and a new sense of purpose filled him.

'Come on, Jem. You're all dressed up. You can't bail now.'

Jemima eyed Laurence without reacting. He was right. In the suite of this fine London hotel, in a vintage gown she'd fallen in love with years ago, she knew she couldn't let Laurence down. Even when all she wanted to do was curl up on the huge bed and stare at the wall.

Just as she'd been doing for five weeks.

Five weeks?

It felt like five years.

When Cam had died, someone had told her that time healed all wounds, and she'd clung to that as a child. She'd truly believed that she might feel less pain as time went on. And in some ways, she had. She thought of her brother every day, she wondered what his life would have been like if he'd lived, but she didn't cry like she used to. Now, she thought of him with a smile, remembering all the ways he'd made her laugh.

Would it be like that with Cesare? Would she

one day be able to disentangle this pervasive sense of hurt from all the lovely memories she had? Would she be able to cherry-pick her way through their time together and see only the parts she wished to recall?

'He's not going to be here,' Laurence chided gently. 'I spoke to his secretary a week ago and she was adamant he couldn't make it. You're not going to run into him at the party.'

Jemima's eyes shifted to Laurence's. She'd been selective in what she'd told him about her time with Cesare. 'A fling,' was how she'd described it. 'Just a fun way to pass some time.' It had taken every scrap of energy she had to present a brave face to Laurence, but she was glad she'd done it.

She didn't want him bearing even a hint of guilt over this—he deserved none, but she knew he'd feel it regardless.

'I don't care if he is,' she lied haltingly.

'Sure you don't.' Laurence's laugh was sympathetic. 'Come on. Come for an hour. Drink some champagne. Dance. Be happy, please.'

Her heart turned over in her chest. 'Am I really so bad?'

'You're miserable,' he said earnestly, so

handsome in his tuxedo. He lifted a hand and brushed her cheek. 'This is our triumph. I want you there with me. It wouldn't feel right without you.'

She smiled, but her chest was hollow because the celebration was, for Jemima at least, tainted by the knowledge she was privy to.

Cesare had, of course, been right. Two weeks after she'd returned from Isola Giada, Laurence had called, out of breath with excitement, to say one of the Silicon Valley tech companies in which he'd invested twelve months earlier had just gone viral—its worth had trebled.

She had no idea how Cesare had foreseen that, but he had. He'd known that night at dinner, and he'd known four weeks later when she'd gone to him and begged him to follow through with the purchase.

He'd used her, and the worst of it was he'd told her as much. Not in so many words, but again and again he'd talked about his desire to win, to succeed at all costs, and she hadn't seen that as a warning—she hadn't heeded it at all.

Even knowing that, she couldn't shake her grief. Because it didn't change a damn thing.

She loved him.

One deed didn't define a person.

Besides, she felt an overarching sadness for him. A sadness that he wouldn't see how much he had to offer. He should have asked her out on a date and she'd have said yes.

Except he hadn't wanted to date her. He hadn't wanted anything other than sex, she reminded herself firmly.

'One hour,' Laurence promised, putting a hand on Jemima's back and gently propelling her to the door.

She swallowed, wishing she could tell him she really would prefer to stay on her own, as she had been for five long weeks.

But Laurence was right. This would be good for her, and at some point she had to stop being a hermit and get back into the swing of things.

'He definitely won't be there?'

Laurence stopped walking, his expression showing more sympathy, so she tried to paste a bright smile to her face.

'What did that bastard do to you?'

'Nothing,' she muttered, shaking her head. She'd styled her hair into a chignon, but her fringe fell over one eye. 'It would just be kind of awkward, that's all.'

'He won't be there.' Laurence's tone showed he wasn't buying her act.

She needed to try harder. 'Okay. Let's go.'

Pausing to check her lipstick in the mirror and grab her clutch, she slipped her arm into the crook of Laurence's. They were on one of the top floors of the hotel, and the ballroom was several floors down. The lift hurtled them there with elegant efficiency, and as soon as the doors opened the noise was deafening. A band was playing crooning jazz songs, and at least two hundred guests were packed into the beautiful, historical room.

Jemima stopped walking, her heart in her throat.

'What is it?' He was so solicitous, she felt like a complete cow for how self-absorbed she'd been. Even his triumph had become about her.

'Laurence, I'm really so proud of you. Look at what you've done.' She gestured towards the ballroom. 'You said you were onto a winner and you were right.' She smiled at him, then lifted up to press a kiss against his cheek.

He grinned, lopsided and so handsome, reminding her for a second of Cam with his cheeky eyes. 'Thanks, Jem.'

The party was filled with investors, some of Europe's wealthiest business people milling about in couture, chatting loudly. But Jemima was internationally known, and her entrance caused a different kind of stir. She was conscious of the eyes that followed her around. She was used to that kind of attention, but she hadn't banked on how difficult it would be to keep up the veneer of happiness, knowing that she was being watched. Fortunately, she found a friend of Laurence's she knew quite well and latched onto him, keeping the conversation light and superficial, so her mind was barely engaged.

When he asked her to dance, she agreed, if only because it would take a few more minutes out of the hour she'd promised Laurence, and she desperately wanted it to be over.

She was weary beyond bearing.

He watched her until he couldn't bear it. He watched her dance, smile, her eyes lifting to whoever the hell was holding her so close to his goddamned body, and he gripped his hands into fists at his side, his expression like thunder so that no one dared approach him. He watched her and he felt as though he was going to punch someone or something.

Fury lashed at his spine, but he knew he didn't have any right to feel like this. He'd told her there was no hope for them. He'd sent her away rather than admit there was any possibility they could be more to one another.

This was his choice. All of it.

He watched her dance and felt as though he was being lit on fire.

With a growl, he stalked from the ballroom, pressing his back to the darkly painted wall opposite, his eyes trained on the door.

He would stand here and he would wait. God help him if she emerged with the other man. What if they were seeing each other? Sleeping together?

His fist pumped. Insanity seemed to burst inside him.

He could picture her body, but never with any one else. It wasn't possible.

Time dragged. He contemplated going back into the party, but he knew it wasn't wise. If she was still dancing with the guy—hell, kissing him—then he wasn't sure he could contain his reaction.

And so he waited, the burgundy carpet of the hotel somehow irritating even though it was an inanimate object.

He waited, and every time the doors opened he leaned forward, away from the wall. The first time it was a couple, too busy making out to notice he was there. The next time it was an elderly man, hobbling with the aid of a cane towards the lifts. Then, another couple, and following that a mother with a small child.

When the door next opened, he didn't hold any hope, which made it all the more shocking to see her.

He stood straight, his eyes drinking her in. She was alone. His body rejoiced. But she was miserable. His insides rolled. She looked…

Broken.

The word breathed through him accusingly. He stayed exactly where he was, watching as she walked past, her head dipped forward, her forehead crinkled, her eyebrows knitted together, her expression so completely distracted. She sashayed as though she were on a catwalk, but he knew her well enough to know it wasn't intentional. She wasn't even conscious that she did that—it was an ingrained elegance she carried with her all the time.

God, he knew that about her, and everything else.

Why hadn't he realised what was happening? How come he hadn't realised that every night they'd spent together had embedded a part of her inside him?

She'd realised. She'd known. And she'd tried to make him understand that, but he'd been so damned determined.

She stopped walking and he held his breath. She stopped walking and stood perfectly still, her head bent, and then she shook it slowly from side to side before starting to walk once more.

His chest lurched.

She approached the lift, pressed her finger to the button and then stepped back. Only once the doors opened and she disappeared inside did he move. His stride was long and urgency propelled him to move quickly. Nonetheless, he only just made it, sliding his fingers into the steel doors as they were almost completely closed. They sprang open, and Jemima lifted her gaze slowly, and then made a groaning noise, shaking her head and stepping backward, as if he was the last person she'd expected to see.

His breath was ragged, torn from him. He stared at her for several long seconds and she stared back. And then she shook her head, as though she could send him away, or maybe pretend he didn't exist. Keeping his eyes on her, he swiped his key against the dashboard and pressed the button for the top floor. She stayed right where she was, staring at him, her features tight, her eyes heavy on his face.

The lift lurched to life. She lifted her hands and curled them around the railing, as though she might fall.

'Is it you?'

His gut churned.

'I don't… You're not… You weren't going to be here.'

Her words rang with accusation. He bit back a curse. He hadn't planned to come. He hadn't, for a second, thought she would know that, nor that she'd make her plans around it.

Had she chosen to attend the celebration because she thought he wouldn't be there?

Could he blame her?

'Change of plans.'

'Oh.' She nodded, frowning, and jerked her head towards the control panel. 'Can you press number twelve, please?'

He thought about refusing. He thought about lifting her against him and holding her until the lift stopped at his floor, carrying her into his room, placing her down on the floor in front of him and talking to her until she understood.

But he'd done enough damage here. This was about fixing things, not making them worse.

He jabbed his finger into the button, and the lift stopped almost immediately, the doors pinging open.

She pushed up from the back of the lift. 'Excuse me.' He stepped out of the lift to make way for her, keeping his hand against the doors for her.

She moved past without looking at him, her back ramrod-straight, her shoulders squared, and he felt a lurch of self-disgust. She was hurting because of him. He watched her for several seconds with a growing sense of consternation and then he began to move after her. She didn't realise until she reached her hotel door, perhaps sensing he was still there, a safe distance behind her.

She whirled around, and now when she spoke her voice was infused with an almost primal frustration. 'What are you doing, Cesare? Why are you here?'

She was hurting, and it was because of him. He closed the distance between them, but didn't touch her. He couldn't. He had no right. 'I came to see you.' The admission was gruff.

'No.' She spat the word at him emphatically. 'Absolutely not.'

'Just to talk,' he said gently, even as panic was spreading through him. 'For a moment.'

'No.' A whisper now, hollowed out.

'Please.' His voice rang with urgency, and her head jerked a little, disbelief in her features. She was going to say no, and God, what would he do then?

He'd come here knowing she might tell him to go to hell, and he had his answer prepared: he was already there.

But Jemima wasn't like that. She didn't have it in her. She was entirely decent and kind, and far fairer than he deserved.

'Two minutes,' she said firmly, pushing the door open and giving him a wide berth. 'And then you get the heck away from me.'

CHAPTER FOURTEEN

'I'M NOT KIDDING, CESARE. Two minutes. Stop standing there and tell me what you want.'

She was shaking like a leaf. She just hoped he couldn't tell. There was a part of her that was terrified she'd hallucinated him. She'd been thinking of him as she'd left the party. Dancing in another man's arms had made her ache for him in a way that had blindsided her.

And then, all of a sudden, he was in the lift with her, surrounding her with his masculine scent, filling her tummy with butterflies and her veins with flame, and all she'd wanted to do was hurl herself at him and tell him she'd do whatever he wanted if it meant she got a little more time with him. Thank God she hadn't. Thank God she remembered what the last five weeks had been like—no way could she do anything that would set her back.

She crossed her arms over her chest, glaring

at him with all the emotional energy she felt, deep in her body.

'How are you?'

She rolled her eyes. 'Fine. Is that it?'

'No.' He moved closer, and she started turning away from him, stalking deeper into her hotel room. She flicked the kettle on and stayed near it, bracing herself in the small kitchen.

'I wanted to see you.'

Something inside her snapped. Her self-control, her temper, something.

'It's been *five weeks*,' she almost shouted.

'I'm aware of that.' His Adam's apple bobbed as he swallowed.

'So what do you want?' She grabbed for a tea cup, slamming it down noisily on the marble bench. 'Let me guess. If I have sex with you tonight you'll give me—what?—a diamond necklace? An Italian villa? What exactly is my price these days?'

He visibly winced, and that empowered her. She liked it. 'Or do you want two nights? Three? It'd cost more for that, you know. At least an aeroplane.' She tore the top off a teabag envelope, shooting him a furious glance as she upended the bag into the mug.

'You have every right to be angry,' he said quietly, and his calmness was like fuel being doused over her fire.

'Damn straight I do! I don't want you to be here! I didn't want to see you again! For five weeks I have felt… I've been…' She shook her head—there were no words that would do justice to how she'd felt. 'And now you're here, looking at me like—I don't even know—and I just… I can't do this. Do you have any idea what this is like? What these five weeks have been like?' She swallowed, her throat thick and dry. 'Please, just leave me alone.' Tears streamed down her cheeks. She reached for the kettle, filling the mug and gratefully lifting it towards her lips.

'And I will,' he promised, moving to the other side of the kitchen bench. She was glad there was some distance between them. She needed that in order to be able to think.

'Please just go.'

'I have one minute left.'

Strength rallied in her core, so she glared at him. 'So use it.'

'I don't know what it's been like for you, but I can tell you what it's been like for me.'

She didn't want to hear, though. She shook her head, sipping her boiling-hot tea, her body barely able to contain her blood, it was rushing so hard and fast.

'I went to Alaska. To work. To think. To make sure I didn't weaken and contact you. There's no phone service there, and you were a million miles away from me. I went to forget you, and instead Alaska became an echo chamber of my thoughts and wants. You were everywhere I looked—in my dreams, my head, my blood, my body—and I needed, simply, to hold you.'

She ground her teeth together, refusing to be placated by his words. 'Like I said, one last night? What's my price?'

He flinched. 'You have no price. You can't be bought. Money had nothing to do with us, with what we were. You knew that all along, and perhaps I did too, on some level, but it comforted me to see a commercial aspect to our arrangement. Commerce I am familiar with and good at. If we were simply a different kind of business deal, I could understand how to get you out of my head. I thought I'd be able to work to the terms we'd agreed, just like any other deal. But I was so wrong.'

Against her will, without her permission, his words seeped under her skin a little. She shook her head, physically rejecting the sentiment. 'No way.'

'No?'

'You can't come here after five weeks, after that last day, and say this and think it makes a damn bit of difference.'

He jerked his head in a silent nod and jagged his fingers in his hair in a gesture that was sheer panic. Good. He should panic!

She sipped her tea. 'Thirty seconds.'

'*Christo*, I'm trying.'

'I'm not messing around, Cesare. You haven't said anything that makes me want to hear more.'

'I was mad with wanting you after that first night. When you came to my office, I saw an opportunity. That's what I'm good at. I see weakness, I exploit it. Your love for your cousin was something I perceived as a weakness, because I'd never really known love like it. I've never known loyalty like it. I couldn't understand what you felt, what motivated you, and so I couldn't see, then, how wrong I was to use it to leverage you into my life.'

'Into your bed,' she corrected succinctly, refusing to feel sympathy for him. 'I was never in your life, really.'

'You were my whole life!' The words were animalistic, thrown at her as though everything he was came down to this moment, to her understanding.

But it had been five weeks, and her hurt went too deep to be eased over.

'That's a load of crap. If I was your life, or any part of it, you would never have let me go.'

He opened his mouth to speak, but she shook her head. 'Time's up. It's my turn. You keep all parts of your life in neat little rows. You tried to do that with me, and when you couldn't you let me go, because you would rather not be with me than risk giving me more of you. You have no idea what these five weeks have been like for me, Cesare, or you wouldn't dare show your face to me. I have been in agony. Every moment has been a torment. I have longed for you with every breath in my body. I have woken up in the middle of the night and reached for you. I have seen you everywhere I go. For two weeks I didn't leave my flat. I have been miserable. *Miserable!*' She roared the last word.

The tirade left her feeling exhausted. She glared at him, though, needing to get through this, and then once she was alone she'd give into the full force of the tears that were threatening to engulf her. 'Please leave.'

'I went to Alaska,' he spoke slowly, as though she hadn't said anything. 'And I caught fish and I ran. I ran as though I could escape you, and I never could, because you're in here.' He pressed his fingers to his chest. 'You followed me everywhere I went, and one day I was running, thinking of you, wondering what you were doing—were you thinking of me? Missing me? Did you still love me? Or had that love turned to hate? And I came upon a grizzly bear. At least eight feet tall, dark brown, easily strong enough to snap me in half.'

Her silence was stony even as her heart was compressing painfully in her chest.

'He was no more than a few feet away and, as he turned to look at me, and I knew I was no match for him—no man could be—I thought that maybe if he were to catch me I would at least be out of my misery. At least I could no longer miss you in a way that was driving me completely insane.'

Another gasp.

'You were right, Jemima. You were so right about me. At sixteen, I swore I would make a success of myself. The memory of how poor my mother and I were has stalked me all my life, and I have done everything I could to outstrip it, to ensure I don't get dragged back into that life. For twenty years I have worked almost every day. I have become singularly determined and utterly stupid, all at once. How could I realise the greatest fortune of my life was standing right before me, begging me to see what we were?'

She squeezed her eyes shut, his words rushing through her.

'I have *never* propositioned a woman for sex. I have *never* blackmailed a woman into my bed. And I have spent the last five weeks wondering why the hell I demeaned myself by behaving in such an outrageous way. And, the truth is, I knew from our first meeting that I couldn't live without you. I didn't know how to win you over with any certainty, and failure wasn't an option, so I did what I could.'

He rounded the kitchen bench, lifting his hands to cup her cheeks. 'I didn't know what it was. I didn't know why I felt this way, I didn't know why a beautiful little bird of a woman had begun to monopolise my every thought and dream. *Christo, uccellina*, I get it now—I get it. Please fly back into my world.'

She shook her head, because she didn't know what she wanted or what she could offer. She just felt completely blindsided.

'I will work, every day, to earn back your trust. I will listen to you next time you try to tell me how I feel. I will do whatever you require of me, but please, do not make me leave now.'

She lifted her face to his, staring at him with a frown on her face. 'I only ever wanted one thing from you.' She spoke quietly, softly. 'I wanted to love you. It was simple, really.'

'No one's ever loved me,' he said. 'So, to me, it wasn't simple. It was terrifying.'

'Why?' She shook her head, still fighting him, fighting this, even when her heart and body wanted her to surrender to what he was offering.

'I have had a long time to think about that, too.' He moved to her again, and she didn't step away. 'My mother almost lost her job because of me. As a child, one day I got into a fight with one of the children she cared for and, when I was disciplined and he was not, I went to the tennis court and I chipped up the grass, right in the middle.' He winced. 'I was sent away to boarding school—my mother's boss pulled some strings and got me a scholarship. I was only a little boy still and the bottom fell out of my world.'

Jemima sucked in a deep breath of air.

'I was made very aware of the fact that I was there by the good grace of the school. If my grades slipped, even a little, I was out. I didn't feel I was welcome at the house my mother worked at—I had no home, and no one. And so I devoted myself to my studies. I worked harder than anyone else at school, and have done all my life. And then I poured that into business. It's driven by a need to succeed, *certamente*, but more than that it's a fear I have, deep down, that if I don't do everything right, everything's going to fall apart.'

He cupped her cheeks. 'No one has ever wanted me for *me*, Jemima. It has been my grades and then my wealth—what I can offer. You are the first person to see me as valuable for who I am, and do you know how terrifying that is? You offered me so much—your beautiful, kind heart—and yet what if I don't deserve it? What if you realise that and I lose you? I don't know how to keep you.'

She sobbed then, a sob for her own sadness, but mostly for his, for the little boy he'd been who'd ceased to recognise his own value. 'Do you love me?'

He lifted his head, a frown on his face. 'Isn't it obvious?'

She smiled, because it was, yet she needed him to say it. 'Not to me.'

'I love you, *sì*. I have loved you, I think, for as long as I have known you.'

'Then keep loving me and you will never lose me.' She lifted up onto her tiptoes so she could brush her lips against his cheeks. 'And don't ever, ever hurt me like that again.'

He grabbed her shoulders, holding her away from him a little so he could look at her properly.

'I won't.' It was so simple, so *him*, and she believed him.

She closed her eyes for a moment, letting the truth of this wash over her.

'I love you,' he said simply. 'And I am terrified that one day you will decide you don't love me. But if the alternative is that I go and wave myself around in front of grizzly bears, then I would rather take this risk, throw myself at your feet and beg you to love me for as long as that good heart of yours can bear.'

'I will love you for ever,' she promised, wrapping her arms around his waist. 'Because that's exactly what you deserve.'

Their kiss swallowed most of his groan.

'You'll marry me?'

She laughed, because it was so like him to ask in such a manner, but she nodded anyway, smiling up at him. 'As soon as humanly possible.'

His eyes flared. 'Done.'

'On one condition.'

He stilled, wariness in him, and she ached to wipe that away. But she knew only a lifetime of being loved and accepted would do that. She smiled, so he knew she was joking, and he relaxed.

'Name it.'

'No way will my husband be able to work the

hours you do. I expect you to take weekends off, at least.'

He grinned. 'I'm going to spend at least the first year of our marriage working from home. And even then, only sparingly. I have executives, you know, and a very wise woman once suggested I should delegate a little more freely.'

'She sounds inspired.' Jemima batted her lashes.

'She is perfect, in every way.'

'And she's all yours, for always.'

'I have a wedding present for you.'

Jemima stifled a yawn against the back of her hand. It was late. Somewhere around two in the morning. Their wedding, in the gardens of Almer Hall, had been everything she could have wanted. Small, no more than thirty people, in a marquee in the garden surrounded by candles and flowers, it had been low-key and exquisite all at once.

He'd flown them via helicopter back to London, and they were now in his townhouse where she'd come that first night—which felt so very long ago now.

'I don't need anything.'

'I know.'

'Then don't give it to me,' she teased, moving across the carpeted room and brushing a kiss against his lips.

He smiled down at her then strode towards the dressing table. He'd taken off his tuxedo jacket and waistcoat and rolled the sleeves of his white shirt up to reveal perfectly tanned forearms that made her mouth go dry with wanting.

'It's something I bought a while ago, as a point of fact. We can call it a gift, rather than a wedding present, if that helps.'

'It doesn't.'

'Well, I cannot return it.' He shrugged and pulled a small white envelope from the drawer.

It was so tiny, perhaps a card or a photo. Nothing of intrinsic value. Curiosity sparked, she extended a hand and he placed the envelope into her fingertips. She slid her finger under the triangular back and pulled out a single sheet of folded paper.

It was the deed for Almer Hall.

'I don't understand.'

He came to stand beside her and pointed to a line at the bottom. *Unencumbered.*

A shiver ran along her spine. She lifted her gaze to his face, incredulity on her features. 'Cesare...' Her voice held warning.

But he pressed a finger to her lips, silencing her, and dropped his hand to another line on the deed. Her eyes followed the gesture and it was then that she read the date—the very same day she'd left the island.

'You did this after we fought?' she whispered, emotions rioting beneath her skin.

'I did it before I propositioned you,' he said. 'I had no intention of leaving your family property debt-ridden once I knew the extent of your worries. I wanted you to stay with me, but I was always going to do this. No matter what.'

Tears filled her eyes. He shook his head gently. 'No more tears, Jemima. This is good news. Your parents don't have to worry. You don't have to worry.'

'I know.' She still couldn't make sense of this. 'So you did this *before* you spoke to me?'

'I think even I knew I was going too far,' he grunted.

'Well, I guess that's something.' She looked at the paper again. 'You didn't have to do this.'

He frowned. 'Yes, I did. You needed help, and I could give it.'

Her heart turned over in her chest.

'Anyway, we are family, and one day our children will want to see their family home.'

'Look at you, taking to the aristocratic life-style,' she teased.

'Never!' He laughed, pulling her to his body, and she couldn't help think how well they fit together. His lips claimed hers and she sighed, surrendering to his kiss most willingly. But when his hands found the waistband of her simple going-away outfit, she pulled away from him.

'Hang on,' she murmured. 'I happen to have a wedding present for you, too.'

'Oh?' He lifted his brows enquiringly.

'But it's not ready yet. It's on back order. It won't be delivered for around seven months or so.'

'What is it?'

'I don't know for sure,' she said, tilting her head to one side.

'My beautiful Mrs Durante, you are making no sense.'

'Aren't I?'

'Something you've ordered, but you don't know what it is?'

'Oh, I didn't order it.' She batted her lashes. 'I think it was more your doing than mine.'

'I don't…'

And then, as comprehension dawned, his hands rushed to cover her stomach. 'You're not…do you mean…?'

She dipped her head forward, pressing her brow to his flat chest. 'Yep.' And then she jerked her face towards his, trying to read his expression. 'Is that… Are you…happy?'

He stared at her, bemused. 'Am I happy?'

She waited, her breath held, her body perfectly still.

'In one night, I have gained as my wife the woman I am head over heels in love with, and now you tell me I am going to become a father? *Sì*, I am happy. I am happier than I ever thought I would be, and it is all because of you. Everything good in this world is because of you, *uccellina*.'

* * * * *